OPERATION: SQUARE PEG

By
IRVING W. LANDE
and FRANK BELKNAP LONG

ARMCHAIR FICTION
PO Box 4369, Medford, Oregon   97501-0168

*For more information about Armchair Books and products, visit our
website at…*

www.armchairfiction.com

Or email us at…

armchairfiction@yahoo.com

EARTH'S HEAD ON THE CHOPPING BLOCK!

It had been a long, destructive interplanetary war, costing countless lives; but Earth's distinguished military forces had finally seemed to gain the upper hand over the invading alien hordes. This success was short-lived, however; one day the enemy introduced an amazing new weapon, a weapon that caused Earth's space pilots to succumb to wild, irrational fears—all while in the midst of combat.

Soon this new secret weapon had turned outer space into a dangerous, pilot-destroying battleground, and it threatened to turn the tide of war in the enemy's favor. With their backs against the wall, the forces of Earth had to find an effective counter weapon. The biggest problem, though, was finding it in time!

FOR A COMPLETE SECOND NOVEL, TURN TO PAGE 127

CAST OF CHARACTERS

ALAN KERR
Earth science had to figure out a way of stopping the Enemy's "fear factor," and he was the man saddled with the job.

FRANCIS GARVEY
He hated everything and everybody—murder ran through his veins—which was why he ended up as a space fighter pilot!

ANN FITZGERALD
She had the misfortune of falling in love with one of Earth's most important scientists—right in the middle of a space war.

DR. MURCHISON
It wasn't his idea—putting hardened criminals into spaceships to fight the Enemy—but he was the one who had to approve it.

PAUL COULTER
One of Earth's best space jockeys. But why were he and other brave pilots turning to raw cowardice in the face of the Enemy?

NICK TABOR
He was a punk, a no-good JD without any respect for the world he lived in—and his best friend made him look like a saint.

FREDDY WILLS
A weak follower with no will of his own—which is why he went along with his pals when they decided to steal an atomic bomb!

CHAPTER ONE

THE ship came in very fast, on the angular zigzag course that was characteristic of autopilot homing. It flipped itself end to end, and backed up to the orbit station on a cushion of bright blue flame. The fires died abruptly, leaving an inert cylinder of dull metal drifting slowly away. Against the blackness of space the ship glowed with a pale but ominous glow, as though it had a very real and vital life of its own.

To the watching men inside the station, the pale glow only confirmed what the mechanical abruptness of the ship's approach had already told them. They watched in grim fascination as the Decon squad went about its business—four men, floating down the life-support energy shaft like fireflies, their legs and arms whirling about.

Presently two sheet-covered bodies were brought back to the station, and the ship moved off to join three others a few hundred yards away, trailing along in a decontamination orbit, like tin cans tied to a dog's tail.

Throughout the station, heads bowed as the commander went outside to read the simple words of the spacemen's funeral service. He touched off the emergency rocket on each suit, saluting the dead men as they moved back and down, starting the long fall home. *Dust thou art, and to dust returneth...*

Back inside, the commander sat down wearily at the tiny desk beside his cot, opened the logbook of the stricken ship, and thumbed through to the last page. He could almost feel the agony of foreknowledge touching his brain, penetrating its twin hemispheres like a white-hot needle. Another ship would become a pilotless coffin...and another...and another. He could only wait—and hope...

5

Operation:

It was a miserable day outside, gray, with a biting damp wind whipping up the Charles. Dr. Alan Kerr pulled his collar tight as he walked over to the bridge. He tried the fast belt three times, and three times was driven back by the wind. Finally he retreated to the stroller, and rode the

Square Peg

A COMPLETE SCIENCE FICTION NOVEL

The Enemy's secret weapon had turned Space into a deadly, pilot-destroying battleground. There had to be a counter weapon. . . . The problem was to find it!

by IRVING W. LANDE and FRANK BELKNAP LONG

endless diagonal sweep across the river, glowering alternately at the ugly water below, and the gloomy outbound mass of tiny cars, cursing the weather and the politicians. The City Council had been arguing about enclosures for the walkalators when he had arrived in Boston nearly three years ago, and the debate was still going on.

By the time he got off the belt it was raining—a cold slanting rain. He was grateful when he reached the ancient apartment house on Commonwealth Avenue, where Ann Fitzgerald shared a comfortable third-floor suite with two roommates.

Ann was assistant to the president of Propulsion Fuels Incorporated, a young sleeper of a firm, only six years old and climbing past the forty million-dollar a year mark. He had met her a year before, while she was taking her master's in business administration at Boston University. She had come up after his lecture on Unconscious Factors in Leadership to ask some penetrating questions, and had remained to join him for coffee, and to listen to an earnest monologue concerning his pet ideas on the real nature of the healing process in psychotherapy.

Since then, he'd been seeing her more and more often, pleased and somewhat surprised to find a girl who didn't get on his nerves and vice versa after two or three months. He'd gotten into the habit of spending Saturday evenings with her—either to go out to a show, or to sit in and talk.

Ann opened the door to his ring, with a bowing gesture like an Elizabethan page. "Hi darling. How are the test tubes today?"

He stepped inside, amused as always at the way the gleaming metal and glass of the PV towered by the fireplace, a strange interloper from the future in this comfortable old room.

Ann took his coat and kissed him lightly on the cheek. A rather slender girl she was, wearing the almost serious expression of a kindergarten teacher. Very light hair, and eyes deeply, incredibly blue. She was wearing a pale blue sweater and a skirt of some dark tweed, and she was the most welcome thing he'd seen all week. As he patted her on the shoulder, the fatigue of a long day with the Screep, the frightening new problems, all faded away in the pleasure of touching her. They stood for a moment motionless, and looked unfocussed into each other's eyes.

Ann said: "I hope you're not reading my mind now."

He smiled. "Don't have to. All I have to do is read my own." He smiled at her affectionately, walked over and dropped to the sofa facing the massive fireplace. "Just let me look at you for a while and forget my troubles."

"Okay darling." She found a bottle of Chianti and poured him a glass. He sipped and watched her as she brought things out from the kitchenette, setting the table for dinner.

Gradually his tension eased away. By the time she announced dinner, he felt more like talking.

She took a sip of Chianti, and picked up the conversation as though there had been no pause. "What kind of troubles do you have today? Are they giving you beautiful female specimens to experiment on?"

He leaned forward, his face sobering. "That would really be trouble," he said. "We learned today we haven't been doing as well as we thought. There was a meeting at the labs this morning. A big one. Two admirals, a couple of cabinet secretaries, and enough Phi Beta keys to start a locksmith's shop.

"They informed us the Enemy pulled a new one out of their hats. It seems they've found a way to slow our crews down. There's been a frightening shift in our casualty figures in the last few months. Up to the beginning of April, we were getting five of their ships for every two or three we lost. We were sitting pretty—reasonably pretty, anyway, if you have to fight a war.

"Since then they've been cleaning house on us. They matched us almost exactly ship for ship, until last month. Then they started going ahead. Last week was really bad. We lost eight ships to get three. Pilot fatigue has been increasing at the same rate as our losses. New pilots, right along with the old ones.

"And this morning, the navy finally got around to telling us about it. Naturally, we'd be the last ones they'd tell. When anything seems pretty ghastly to them, they keep it under wraps as long as possible."

Ann's levity had dropped away. "Do they know what's causing it?"

"That's what has them stumped. Our pilots are convinced they're better trained than the enemy. Our radar is two hundred miles better than theirs. Of course, their ships are a little lighter—they can stay out longer and travel a little farther on a mission. But in a fight, that hardly ever makes any difference. It can be written off as negligible."

"Could it be sabotage?" Ann asked. "Or maybe it's just a temporary change in the figures—tired pilots—tired ships?"

Alan shook his head emphatically. "That's what they hoped for a while. But this thing has gone beyond all possible chance of becoming explicable as just a temporary shift in the fortunes of war. The engineers have gone over the ships inch by inch. They've tested them as though they had just come off the drawing boards. And they swear the ships are as good as ever—better, in fact. The only real clue we have is in this note. They found it in the logbook of a ship that came home on auto. The pilot was dead; navigator dying."

Alan reached into a jacket pocket and skimmed an envelope onto the table.

He stared sourly at the fireplace as Ann extracted a crumpled logbook page from the envelope. The aura of a soldier's death agony hung in the room as she read.

We're dead. We got the bastard, but he broke in our direction and our bomb followed him. Got caught in the edge of the explosion—took a mess of radiation...

"Radio out, ship is on auto for orbit station. Hope you can clean it up and use it again. She's a good boat.

"Figure I have ten or fifteen minutes, and there's something I want to say. The Enemy has something that's making us look awful bad. Something that scares us. Noticed it in the last six or eight fights. The closer we got to them, the scareder I got. Different from the usual scared because it's a fight. Out of proportion somehow. First times I just felt gloomy, slow, uneager—figured I was just getting a bellyful. But each time it went deeper like it was adding up. Like sandpapering the skin on your fingers. Each time more scared—harder to keep mind on the

fight. Not scared of fight—just scared, period.

"Ask other guys. They won't admit it unless you ask—ashamed to admit scared but they know. Make 'em talk, they'll tell you...

"Tell Bill Wylie say goodbye to Susie for me. Tell her I'll—"

Ann folded the note almost tenderly, and placed it carefully in the envelope before she looked up. "What does it mean, Alan?"

"It means they're beating us at our own game. They're outgunning the Screep."

She frowned. "I don't understand. How can they get to a man on a spaceship equipped with a Screep?"

"That's what has us worried. Actually, it wouldn't be a Screep—just based on the same ideas, but a lot farther along. We've been worried about something like this, ever since they pulled most of the good Human Resources men off research, and dumped the budget into Screep training. But the way the battle scores were going, we had to keep quiet. Now we've been topped, and I think we're in for a nasty time."

Ann leaned over absently, to brush a stray lock off his forehead. "Well, as long as there isn't any real war, you'll have time to figure out what they're up to."

"That's just the point, Ann!" He slammed his fork down. "It *is* a real war! The only reason we haven't been fighting here on Earth is that we've been so evenly matched out there. Neither of us can set up a moon station because the other would blow it to smithers. The minute the Enemy controls space, we'll be politely invited to join their fifteen-nation team—on *their* terms. And if they have the muscles to back up the invitation, we'll think very seriously of joining without firing a single bomb.

"This is very likely all the war there's going to be. Whoever wins it takes home all the marbles. Don't kid yourself that just because we all pretend nothing is happening out there, it doesn't count. This is for keeps. And the navy had to sit on the thing for four months before they decided maybe they ought to tell us about it!"

CHAPTER TWO

ALAN FINISHED HIS shrimp cocktail; toyed for a moment with his dinner, and got up. He began to walk around the room, hands in pockets, kicking idly at tufts in the rug.

"The answer's in the Screep somewhere. Somewhere there was a turn we missed." He was muttering almost to himself.

Ann glanced unhappily at the plate he had left, then watched him as he punched a fist into the palm of his left hand, scowling down into the fireplace.

"Would you like to tell me about the Screep?" she asked. "Perhaps it would help."

He shrugged. He knew she was cleared for top secret in her job, but for reasons he hadn't cared to explore, he had never felt like talking to her at any length about his work. He did tonight, however.

He shrugged again, and the irritation on his face faded to petulance.

"The thing started in seventy-two, when Sorokin stumbled onto the Resonator. Somebody set a lab rabbit down next to a screwy ultrasonic generator he'd rigged to run up and down the spectrum in an intricate pattern. Sorokin noticed that every once in a while the rabbit would cringe and whimper for a moment. When he noticed that the cringing came at regular intervals, he smelled something big. He went to work with humans—mostly himself.

"In a couple of years he established a wave pattern that stimulated fear, and in another year he had the emotional spectrum. Thinking was much too complicated—still is—but the basic emotions run in patterns that are reasonably constant.

"For a while we worked with just the Resonator—specially tuned, of course. The thing looked like a crazy cribbage board, with dozens of tiny vibrators stuck in it. We actually had a tuning knob with the names of emotions for positions, and a…'volume control'. We found that we could do wonderful things in psychotherapy simply by using it to help hold a man in a problem.

"Then Sorokin and a couple of smart electro-encephalographers came up with the big one—a machine that picked up emotion wave patterns directly from the brain and converted them into the corresponding ultrasonics. Theoretically, all it meant was that with a pair of these gadgets, the patient and therapist could transmit their emotions to each other, and generate real empathy. And it worked. Psychotherapy got sharper, finer, and faster in every respect. Diagnosis began to mean something more than just cataloging what we didn't know.

"But something else happened, too. Gradually we learned—it's hard to explain—that we could do more than merely create a resonated emotion in the patient. We could actually feel where the bodies were buried. We could tell what the patient was unconsciously avoiding—and how to create an emotion—slightly different—that would sort of nudge him in the right direction. And with the therapist 'plugged in' as a kind of condenser, taking the overloads, the patient was able to tackle and reduce problems he couldn't have handled alone, no matter how sympathetic or wise the therapist might be. It was more like telepathy than the theory would account for."

Ann had stretched herself out on the sofa while he talked, her chin resting in her palms, her eyes following him intently as he paced the carpet. "That was the Screep?"

"That was the Screep. The Sorokin Converter for the

Reproduction of Emotional Energy Patterns. *Quite a gadget.*"

"It must have been tricky learning to use a thing like that," she said.

"We had our troubles," Alan said. "There was one time I was working with a patient who was supposed to be reasonably sound—a few anxieties—that sort of thing. I was just a student at the time. He was talking about some bully who had picked on him in the third grade, so I nudged him with a little fear. The next thing I knew, four of the other students were pulling him off my throat. It took all four of them. If I live a thousand years, I'll never forget the hammer blow of terror and hatred that hit me just before I blanked out."

"I suppose there were other incidents like that."

"There were others, some much worse, but that was the worst I ran into personally. It doesn't take much of that to make you careful."

"And then the navy took it over to train space crews?" Ann asked.

"Yup. It was obvious that the Screep was the best method ever developed for selecting the most stable, alert, obedient men—or men with other special qualities."

Alan began to kick the rug again. "So we became a branch of the Bureau of Human Resources—Screepers!" He bit the word out savagely. "And the basic research just about stopped. We trained space soldiers."

His pacing had taken him to the window, where he stood for a moment watching the treetops whip back and forth in the gathering darkness. When he turned back to the room he was calmer. "Of course, the best soldier isn't necessarily the sanest man. Obedience often conflicts with reason. But in combat, obedience can be survival. They have a saying: 'One poor decision well carried out is better than two good ones argued about.' So we worked out a compromise—so much aggressiveness, so much initiative, so much obedience. And a few other things. It isn't exact, but you'd be surprised at how close we can come."

Her legs flashed as she rolled over on her side, propped up on an elbow, and his eyes widened in appreciation.

"It seems like a very efficient system." She composed her skirt. "Is the Enemy doing it any better?"

"We have no idea, and that's why we're kicking ourselves in the butts. There just weren't enough men left over from the training program to keep pushing the original research. Of course we've improved the Screep, but it's still just a Screep. The most tantalizing thing about this business is that it's so easy to be smug about what you know, because you don't know what you don't know.

"The whole Screep program is based on what amounts to physical contact between the operator and trainee. Ultrasonics don't carry well in air anyway, but this isn't ordinary action at a distance. It's action across a hard vacuum at ranges of several hundred miles. The Enemy has somehow bypassed the ultrasonic wave pattern sequence that will directly stimulate an emotion. And they're using it to trigger disabling fear in our crews." Alan chuckled. "It reminds me of a story they used to tell when I was a kid. About how telegraphy was the same as squeezing a dog's tail here and having him bark in Philadelphia; and radio was the same thing without the dog. That's what we're up against—the same thing without the dog."

She was frowning thoughtfully. "Haven't soldiers always been afraid?"

"Yes, but at a level they can overcome in taking action, and turn into anger. That's the real root of bravery. But this upsets the normal fear-action-bravery sequence. When a man is trying to act and he's still filled with fear, he loses coordination. His effective IQ drops to a small fraction, and he becomes unstable. Back in the early air wars, many crewmen jumped without parachutes from bombers that hadn't been scratched. Fear of dying, and uncertainty—the worst kind of fear—drove them to an illogical suicide. The last couple of minutes of a combat approach require every bit of intelligence and coordination a man possesses. The figures are showing what happens when these factors are reduced."

"But if this thing is electronic, how is it your problem? You're a psychologist."

He smiled. "It doesn't come in neat packages like that. Sure, the physicists and engineers are trying to duplicate the thing—if it is electronic—to fight it on its own level but we don't know how far we're behind. It could take anywhere from a month to years, to find the answers. And we haven't got years. At the present loss rates, we may not even have a year. And there's no guarantee it won't get worse."

The smile left his face. "Unless we can find something at our level—a drug perhaps—something we can do with the Screep to prepare the trainees for...whatever it is. Or maybe a different type of trainee...stolid peasant types, maybe, or even some kind of psychotics...anything that will give them time to work. Otherwise we may never get the other answers. The problem isn't just to catch up with the Enemy. We've got to find a way to control this thing, whatever it is, while we chase them."

He finished beside the sofa and sat down, drawing Ann down beside him and slipping one arm about her waist. "Well, maybe the death ray boys can come up with some way of shielding the ships without fouling up the radar."

Slowly she freed herself and stood up. "It will wait till tomorrow. Let's finish dinner while it's still edible—I hope."

CHAPTER THREE

MORE OFTEN THAN not, the brightest and the darkest strands of human destiny become intertwined simply because a man turns right instead of left on a crowded street, or buys an ill-fitting pair of glasses, or forgets to wind his watch on getting up in the morning. Coincidental threads—trivial in themselves—are caught up and quickly woven into a larger pattern that may loom through the mists of time as a Mt. Everest of human achievement or come to resemble the shadow that falls across a man on the day of his death.

At the very moment when Dr. Kerr was rejoicing in the warmth and sympathetic understanding of Ann Fitzgerald another young man—in another part of Boston—was finishing his dinner under quite different circumstances.

The term 'young man' has very little value in pointing up a comparison and in this particular instance it should perhaps not be used at all. Certainly its use can be justified only in a very broad, generic sense, for Alan Kerr was a mature individual with a great deal of intellectual discernment and Francis Garvey was a teenage hoodlum who hardly seemed to merit the second half of the term.

'Young ape' would have perhaps more suitably described him—if modern psychiatry had been permitted to think in such terms. But fortunately there are stern restraints imposed on what psychiatrists may think, and the average, well-informed practitioner would have preferred to take a second look at what made Francis Garvey run.

By night and by day inside Garvey the jungle waged unceasing warfare. And since there was no censor, no psychological block, in Garvey's mind all the struggle took place at all levels and frequently at the very perimeter of his consciousness.

Each encounter was waged with a savage cruelty and a savage cunning. But there could be no hope of eventual victory, because in such a mind the jungle wars only against itself. How could it be otherwise when every member of a wolf pack is exposed to constant treachery from within, and there is no reason to choose one night-black thicket above the other, and survival becomes an end in itself?

Francis Garvey—the "Francis" was just one of a thousand cruel affronts inflicted upon him in his infancy—was a good-looking youth with neatly manicured fingernails and features that gave him at times a bland, almost ingratiating aspect. But those same features could become sullen without warning and turn even more quickly into a mask of sneering defiance.

In fact, his eyes—when you looked at them closely—were almost always the opposite of ingratiating. They were too probing and too dark, and though they might have been invaluable to a man in a prosecuting attorney's role they were hardly an asset to Garvey.

"What's troubling you, kid?" Nick Tabor asked, pushing back his plate and surveying the lunch-bus customers with amused tolerance. "If the way that waitress cold-shouldered you ain't acceptable, why don't you just grab her? Or haven't you got a long enough reach?"

"Garve couldn't do that," Fred Wills said, with mock solemnity. "She ain't good looking enough. Garve here is kind of particular."

Wills was a smooth-looking youth, too, with a round baby face that had lost all of its innocence on the day he'd discovered that his parents had no liking at all for the intricacies of child rearing.

"I'm not particular," Garvey said, his dark eyes downcast. "All dames look alike to me."

"What does that mean? You like 'em ugly as well as good

looking? Nick, you hear that? He wants to make love to a girl with no *charm.*"

"Quit needling me, will you? I didn't say anything about making love. I don't want to make love to them or have them make love to me. This love business is only a phony excuse, anyway."

"Look who's talking. I'll bet the guy's never even taken out a hunting license."

"He's got a license—haven't you, Garve?"

"I told you to quit needling me..."

Suddenly the knife snapped open. Garvey had whipped it out so quickly that his companions were caught completely off-guard. Wills recoiled in alarm, his face whitening. Tabor just stared, but a tiny muscle in his jaw began to twitch spasmodically.

It was a big knife, with a white plastic handle and a nine-inch blade. It was a push-button knife—and now it was open and ready.

It was Tabor who spoke first. "What's wrong with you, kid? We know all about your dame record. If it wasn't solid do you think we'd kid you about it. Freddy was talking out of turn. Ain't that so, Freddy."

"Sure it's so. I—I didn't mean a word of it."

"You meant it, all right. And I'll tell you what *I* meant. When I said I wasn't particular I meant—about easy dames. The hard-to-get ones I'm plenty particular about." Garvey snapped the knife shut and returned it to his trousers' pocket. "Okay, forget it."

Wills stared at him in relief. He seemed to be getting a little of his composure back. After a moment he leaned forward and whispered confidentially, "Those hard-to-get dames. Maybe we should do something about that. Is there any one dame in particular—"

"No one dame," Garvey said. "I told you to forget it."

It was something Garvey wanted to forget himself. He'd watched her come out of the Propulsion Fuels Building maybe a dozen times. He'd been on the corner watching after the first time, when he'd seen her come out by accident. There was something about her—

Alone in his room at night he kept remembering how her hips had swayed when she walked. It wasn't a 'put on' strut—not the easy-dame kind of grind at all. It was just an 'all woman' something that made a guy's pulses pound and the blood mount to his temples.

Hell, why should he torture himself? There were plenty of other women just as desirable—and not all of them were so high above him either. He could reach right up into a Cadillac if he wanted to—

"Come on, let's go," Tabor said, rising abruptly from the long counter and giving Garvey's elbow a nudge. "Just talking about chicks ain't getting us nowhere. If you liked that waitress you could stay here and make progress. But you don't like to talk to her back. That I can understand."

"Where'll we go?" Wills asked. "Got anything in mind?"

"Haven't I always," Tabor said.

"But where—"

Tabor grinned.

"Well, there's a feelie-talkie playing at the New Lyceum tonight that should take our minds off the War. One of these days a recruiting sergeant's going to reach out and take us right off the hook. There'll be no chicks to worry about then. I read a book once about a guy who went to Venus and got tangled up with a green woman—green and as naked as a seal. He went walking with her on a beach, and the waves came in pretty like, and all of a sudden she wasn't fighting him off anymore."

"Sure, in a book. But there's no life on Venus or any of the planets. What a way for things to turn out."

"What did you expect? Aren't there enough dames for you right here on Earth? How about it, kid? Aren't there enough?"

"Too many," Garvey said. "But that recruiting sergeant stuff is the bunk. They won't take me. I've got too many short raps chalked up against me. Add helicab stealing to shaking down bookies and making passes at dames who don't know when you're doing them a favor—"

"Sure, I get it. It adds up to a big rap—to one big rap. And they won't take a guy in the Space Force who'll contaminate every ugly son in a cootie-barracks by teachin' them how to put the squeeze on the hopped up brass. Me, I don't have to worry either. I got a blown-out right eardrum."

"That ain't what you just said," Wills protested. "About the recruiting sergeant taking us off the hook—"

"I was really thinking about *you*, Freddy. Garve here has an out—and so have I. But there's nothing to stop them from taking you. What's one short stretch on a reform farm? They'll take you and make a man out of you, kid. Can't you just picture yourself flyin' through space with the greatest of ease with the Enemy getting angrier by the minute.

"First you lose your legs. You think, 'I can get along without legs. Some dames aren't particular that way.' Then—poof! Your arms go too. So you're a basket case. So what? You can still get around inside your head."

"Cut it out," Garvey said. "There's a lot of guys inside those big ships. The ship gets blown apart—you get blown apart with it. It all happens so fast you don't feel nothing. You don't just get your butt singed."

"I bet you'd be scared though," Wills said. "A few seconds before it happens—"

Garvey's eyes darkened.

"That's what *you* think. You're the quick-hollerin' kind. You should carry a can of preservative to put your guts in.

Not too big a can—because then all you'd see would be a floating speck."

Wills' face flushed. "That's real crazy talk. If a punk kid said that to me I'd flatten him out. But you're supposed to be my pal—"

"You mentioned being scared. I just don't like to hear guys talk chicken, that's all."

"You don't want anybody to say what he thinks—is that it?"

"You didn't say *you'd* be scared. You said *I'd* be scared. When an idea like that pops into your head—keep it to yourself."

"Sure, Garve. I only—"

"Shut up! I ought to whack you on the can!"

"What you guys both need is something to cool you off," Tabor said. "That talkie-feelie I told you about ought to do it." Tabor framed his hands in the air like a movie screen. "Laura La Rouche in 'Lisbon Express'."

"You mean 'heat us up', don't you?" Wills asked.

"I mean just what I said. You go in heated up and come out cool. That's because it's just about as good as the real thing."

"It's never as good," Garvey said.

"Come on, kid. When you're stretched out in a seat at the Lyceum with 'feelie' cuffs on your wrists you'll change your mind. You'll be holdin' Laura La Rouche in your arms, but she won't be any one special chick. She'll be all chicks rolled into one."

A half-hour later, Tabor's prediction proved true enough—as far as it went. Garvey was taking in what lay within the radius of the deep-view screen with his eyes while his other senses were being stimulated simultaneously. His face was flushed, his breathing fierce and abandoned, and Laura La Rouche was tight in his arms.

But she wasn't really Laura La Rouche. She was every woman he'd ever hated and wanted to hurt. She was every woman he'd ever wanted to cheat and betray, crush and abandon. She was the hateful symbol of something deep within himself that enraged him so much that he could only gain release from his torment by crushing it. That something wasn't a woman at all. In fact, it wasn't even a *something*. It was the *lack* of a something. It was a great, terrible emptiness—a repudiation and an emptiness—where a something should have been.

And the emptiness had so cheated him, had so outraged and hurt him, that he could only find the peace his inflamed mind craved by crushing it.

It was a terrible kind of peace, exacted at a terrible price. He was hurting himself too. He was like a wolf tugging to free its leg from a trap, with a convulsive wrenching of its entire body. He was hurting not only himself, but the whole world. But he wasn't afraid to hurt, hurt, hurt. Hurt and crush. He wasn't afraid. He didn't care.

He could remember how it had been the first time. He'd been too young to really understand, but not too young to feel. The hard, rough hand descending to smite him—on buttocks and thigh. The awful, spinning emptiness of the room, the cracked plaster on the wall, the terrible, accusing, rage-convulsed face of his father.

If his mother had picked him up then and comforted him the emptiness would have become less frightening and he might not have begun to hate at all.

But his mother had gone right up to his father and said: "Next time hit him harder. He's got to be taught a lesson. The ugly, ungrateful brat!"

He had not only wanted to kill his father then. He had hated his mother for refusing him the smallest shred of comfort, for turning on him and screaming at him too. It would have been so easy for him to forgive his mother. But she had never given him a chance to forgive her. She had gone right on siding with his father, year after year.

Garvey's hands were around Laura La Rouche's throat now. It wasn't happening on the screen. He was punishing her in his own secret way, taking his time about it, pressing his fingers deeper and deeper into her windpipe.

He wasn't afraid to do it. No matter what Tabor might have thought—he wasn't chicken when it came to the showdown.

Suddenly his fingers relaxed their grip. Laura La Rouche was now so completely at his mercy that he could afford to be generous, almost kind in his treatment of her. He relaxed his grip and smiled at her. Then he slapped both of her cheeks hard with his balled up fists, and whispered warningly:

"Next time I'll go through with it. You hear what I say? Don't give me any of that soft stuff or there won't be a next time. You thought I'd make love to you, eh? Love—what a laugh! Did you think I'd fall for the kind of bait dames like you use to sucker guys?"

"Hell, what's got into you, Garve," Tabor said. "What are you whispering to yourself for? Sit still, can't you? I came here to enjoy the picture. You'd think you had a chicken by the neck, or something. Whoever heard of wringing a chicken's neck at a Laura La Rouche picture."

"Hey, you'll get us thrown out!" Wills whispered, almost pleadingly.

"It's not a chicken," Garvey said. "Just a chick. A chick who's getting what she deserves."

"What do you mean—what she deserves? Nothing's happened to her yet. She's got three guys crazy about her, which is a pretty good showing for anyone dame. A pretty good showing!"

Garvey removed the 'feelie' cuffs from his wrists and straightened in his seat. "I've seen enough," he said. "I'm going outside for a smoke. If I don't come back in I'll meet you in front of the theater."

"Sure, go ahead. It's all right by me if you want to walk out on the juiciest part of the picture. It's coming along any minute now. She's going to settle for only one guy and concentrate on him. That's when a 'feelie' really pays off. Brother, I may be stuck here all night. I may want to see it over again."

"He means he wants to feel it over again," said Wills, with a quite unnecessarily Rabelaisian candor.

CHAPTER FOUR

GARVEY GOT UP without commenting and walked straight down the aisle and out of the theater into the neon-bright night.

Boston Common was ablaze with lights and there were big colored posters everywhere urging the citizenry to volunteer for the Space Force, and not wait to be drafted. There was a very large one directly opposite the theater and Garvey lit a cigarette and stood studying it for a moment with a triumphant smirk on his lips.

Upstairs, he told himself, there were a lot of saps right now being blasted to bits. It wasn't for him, and never would be for him. Let the other guy stick out his neck.

Garvey had read about seven books in his life. One of them he still remembered. It was by a writer many years dead—Ortel or Orwell or something like that—and it was about what the world was going to be like in about forty years.

Well, the forty years were up and it hadn't come out the way Orwell had predicted it would. There were supposed to be posters everywhere with a frowzy-faced guy in uniform staring out and underneath a warning which read: BIG BROTHER IS WATCHING YOU.

Maybe that would have been good. Maybe someone should be watching, checking up on people. You felt more secure that way. You just let go and let somebody else do all the worrying. *Big Brother is Watching You. Big Brother is Taking Care of You.*

All right. He, Garvey, didn't really want anyone watching him. But there were a hell of a lot of people who could bear watching. The cops, for instance—all of the cops. Get rid of the cops and just have one Big Guy watching. He'd need assistance, of course. But it wouldn't have to be the cops. Mister Big could use guys like Garvey himself—guys who wouldn't take any guff from anyone.

Hell, why not? It would feel good to be on top for a change instead of where he was. He wouldn't have to go around looking over his shoulder because Mr. Big would always be there backing him up. If anyone that Special Assistant Garvey didn't like stepped out of line—*Whamo!*

The cops were afraid to use their nightsticks when it came to a real showdown—especially against teen-agers. But he, Garvey, wouldn't be afraid. He'd even use *his* nightstick—no, it would be a steel-lined head-buster—against dames if they tried to sucker him. Not all dames—just the easy kind. The hard-to-get kind he'd handle in a different way.

Just a nod from him would send them to prison for life. So naturally they'd do everything they could to please him and avoid a fate worse than death.

Why had Orwell made such a wrong guess? Writers were screwy—that was about all you could say about them. Why would anyone want to be a writer in the first place? Practically every day you read about writers starving to death. If a guy couldn't predict right, maybe he deserved to starve.

What it boiled down to was this—the guys upstairs who were fighting the Enemy were saps, writers were saps, the big-mouths were saps—and just about the only sensible guys were guys like Francis Garvey.

But just *try* making the big mouths see that. They were always talking about more playgrounds, more recreational facilities, keep the kids off the streets. Kid stuff. He'd never known the time when he couldn't look after himself. You didn't have to buzz in under the floor to get what you wanted. You could go right out and take it.

That was the trouble with a hunk of filth like Freddy Wills.

He let himself be afraid. He turned chicken the instant he saw a knife with a big blade standing out straight.

You could only die once. It was important to be the first when you saw trouble shaping up—the first to whip out a knife. But say you were a little slow, a little careless about that. You could still charge right into a knife and take it away from the other guy if you were angry enough.

Anger was the important thing. Resenting interference, staying mad.

You know what can happen if you fail, so you don't fail.

Posters on Boston Common—red and blue in the neon flare. *Enlist—Enlist—Enlist. Defend Your Right to Freedom.*

Three ships blasted down—five—fourteen. And high in the sky men are dying. Let your bomb go at a hundred miles—no closer and get out at maximum acceleration. When the pip reaches center watch out. You haven't got all the time in the world, you know.

The Enemy thinks our space station is too close to the moon. Wouldn't you like to change their thinking, chum? Enlist—enlist now. Laura La Rouche is taking the express to Lisbon and you can go with her all the way. That's your privilege as a human being. But it might be better to go out into space right now. How about it, guy?

"You don't know what you missed Garve!" said Tabor, so close to Garvey that he recoiled a step in instinctive resentment, hunching his shoulders and bending an arm to give himself more elbowroom.

Tabor and Wills were well in front of the other emerging patrons but the exit rush was on. Everyone seemed impatient to get out under the neon glare.

"I know what I missed," Garvey said. "Her pictures always end in just one way—with just one guy in trouble."

"She stayed stacked," Wills said. "You got to hand it to her when it comes to loving."

"He started making passes at the air just like you did," Tabor said. "I thought I'd have to chain him to his seat."

"What do we do now?" Wills asked. *"Where do we go?"*

"Look at him, Garve. He ain't satisfied. He holds Laura La Rouche in his arms and now he wants to do something else—for kicks."

"I thought of something," Garvey said. "But maybe you guys haven't got the nerve for it."

"What is it, Garve?"

"How would you like to lift a steel ingot white-hot out of a blast furnace and set it down over there on the Common?"

"You're kidding, Garve."

"Sure I'm kidding. But I've got another idea that's just as good. We take off in one of those recruiting trucks and we lift a chick that's just like an ingot. Then we set her down to cool off somewhere."

"That kind of a chick, eh? Why couldn't we just pick her up with a wolf call?"

"The ride will be for kicks. We've got to shanghai a truck and that won't be easy. You know what they got in some of those trucks? Not just amplifiers, not just recruiting posters. *They got regular spaceship installations.* Small ones—like relays that sound warning horns and close blast doors and start bells ringing. And maybe a little bomb that could go off accidentally—if we're not careful."

"A real bomb? You're kidding."

"No I'm not. I read about it in the tele-tabloids. They want to show the guys down here what it's like up there— give 'em a small sample of the real thing. So what do they do? They don't even take the stuffings out of some of those little bombs. They stand in back of the truck and show them to the guys on the Common. It's safe enough because those bombs don't go off without special equipment—detonators and things. It helps recruiting. The guys read about it in the tele-tabloids just like I did and they know it's a real bomb and that gets 'em all excited."

"They rush in and enlist."

"It figures," Tabor said.

"Sure it figures. But when we get inside that truck we may have to knock a couple of soldiers cold. And those same guards will have their hands on the relays, maybe. Or on the detonating wires or something. So what happens to us? The bomb goes off. It's just a little bomb, but it goes off, and it takes half of the Common with it. It takes us with it. How do you like that?"

"I don't like it," Wills said. "I don't go for it, Garve. I let you talk, because I could see it was on your mind. But why do it? We don't have to blow ourselves up just because an idea sounds like it might be exciting."

Garvey stepped forward and grabbed Wills by his coat-lapels. He brought the lapels tight up around Wills' throat and tugged viciously at the slack. Wills began to choke. His tongue protruded and he got red in the face.

"Goin' chicken again, eh? Ask me pretty what would happen if you got spattered all over the Common. Ask me pretty and maybe I'll tell you. All right, I'll tell you anyway. There wouldn't be any loss to anybody—anywhere."

"Let him breathe, Garve," Tabor said. "What the hell! If a guy is born chicken he stays chicken and that's all there is to it."

"Yeah, but he's going into the truck first. You hear what I say, Freddy? You're going right into that truck with your yellow streak showing. You're goin' to say: 'I'm Freddy Wills, and I want to enlist and be a big brave hero. Don't look at me like that. I was born this way—I can't help it. Can't you guys do something for me? I know how you must feel, looking at a worm like me. But you've got to try to work out something that will give me a chance to be a hero.' "

Garvey released Wills and sent him spinning backwards against the 'feelie-talkie' animation poster on the opposite side of the entrance lobby. Wills collided with the poster and half-clung to it, a pleading desperation in his eyes. Suddenly he was sobbing. Great, convulsive sobs racked him as he clung to the poster.

Above his head Laura La Rouche walked across a terrace high above the Madeira Islands. It was a bright, clear morning and the sea between the islands was azure-blue and ageless and it stretched away into blue distances that made all human grief seem remote and unreal. It was a Homeric-legend sea, and no black warplanes droned above it and it was dotted with tiny red and blue sails all moving in the same direction—toward the sunrise.

And it was easy to see that the terrace was designed only for casual dalliance and there was no reason to suspect that Laura La Rouche would say or do anything that would have to be stricken from the record by stern modern censors, because stern modern censors were conspicuous by their absence.

"You've hurt his feelings, Garve," Tabor said, chuckling softly as he stared. "Why did you have to do that?"

Garvey went up to Wills and patted him on the shoulder. "You're breaking my heart," he said. "It looks like you're all in a dither. When do you think you'll be able to turn off the tears? Take your time. Don't tell me until you're sure. If you turn chicken a third time the knife is goin' to come right up out of my pocket fast. So just make sure, that's all. I hate to see a guy crawling along the pavement with a shiv in his guts, yelling for the cops."

"Let me alone," Wills sobbed. "Take your hands off me. If you try to pull anything—"

"It could happen right here. I know how to get away fast. Maybe that could be our kicks for the evening. Just say the word—"

Wills straightened, his face ashen. "All right," he choked. "I'll go through with it. Don't just press me, that's all."

Garvey turned and walked back to where Tabor was standing, a triumphant smirk on his face.

"All right," he said. "Now we steal a truck. Come on, let's get started."

Night breezes stirred the trees along Boston Common, women laughed and moved closer to their escorts, a jet plane droned overhead. And far away and long ago—a terrifying ten hours ago—the orbit station knew more mourning, knew more grief. The decontamination trail glowed bright against the blackness of space and the commander whispered beside a flag-draped coffin:

"I hope they can do something about it. I know they'll keep on trying. Dr. Kerr's a good man—the right man for the job. I think he'll come up with the answer. Just give him time."

CHAPTER FIVE

ALAN KERR SAT on the sofa in the living room, finishing his third cup of after-dinner coffee. The coffee was very strong and black, the evening still young and by rights he ought to have felt good.

He didn't—and it was only natural perhaps that he should have asked himself why he didn't.

"Ann?" he said.

"Yes, darling, what is it?"

"They say that only a physician can cure the ills of a man's body and only a woman the sickness of his mind. I wonder how much truth there is in that."

She looked at him strangely for a moment, then said: "Are you trying to tell me that you think you are mentally ill?"

"Not exactly," Alan said. "I imagine I could get by in any large company of reasonably well adjusted men. What intolerable restraints society sometimes imposes on men and women whose one, overmastering desire is to live and think creatively. Quite unnecessary restraints—restraints designed to curb the jungle impulses of a very low order of human intelligence."

Alan paused and took a slow sip at his coffee. "The point I really want to make," he continued, "is this…society knows—or senses unconsciously—that the jungle isn't easy to curb. It knows that the jungle is largely dominated by a low order of intelligence. But it also knows that the jungle is hideously complex and dangerous. So what does society do? It imposes restraints to curb—hit-or-miss curbs—and some of them cripple or destroy human creativeness.

"Society has to impose curbs to function at all. That can be taken for granted. But the measure of a society's progress toward greatness is the degree of freedom and independent judgment it allows its best minds to exercise."

"I understand all that," Ann said. "At least—I think I do. What makes you so sure I'm not capable of understanding?"

"I didn't say that. You are capable. But you hold yourself under constraint when emotional out-going becomes imperative. You're afraid to come right out and say: 'Alan, you've had a tough day. Don't let it worry you. I'm right here to cushion the shock. Here are my hands—hold them. I'll run them through your hair if you like.' "

"But darling, I—"

"Wait a minute. Let me finish. Daily I run head on into some of the curbs I've been talking about. I take a terrible pounding from the jungle. Take the whole problem of the Screep. I have my own ideas about the Screep and the men I'm working with have different ideas. Sometimes we agree but more often we disagree. And that's where the jungle starts coming out. That's when you encounter envy, hatred, malice and anger in everyone you meet. And in yourself. The jungle inside you starts fighting back. It takes and gives no quarter.

"Society, you see, just isn't wise enough yet to impose the right kind of curbs and permit the right kind of freedom to men who are fully aware that the exercise of freedom is always a risk, always a danger that can grow cobra-fangs overnight. But you have to be willing—and able—to take that risk. Otherwise we all really will go back into the jungle for keeps."

"I see," Ann said. "Just what is it you want me to do?"

"This," Alan said, getting slowly to his feet. He walked up to her and took her into his arms and kissed her very firmly on the lips.

For an instant her arms went around his shoulders and she responded to his ardor with all the impetuosity that he could have desired. She returned his first kiss long and lingeringly and then she kissed him five or six times very rapidly on every part of his face in a wholly wonderful way.

Then she suddenly stopped kissing him. She seemed to regret letting herself go, and a look of embarrassment and self-reproach came into her eyes. She drew back from him, drew away, and said very quietly and firmly: "You shouldn't have done that, Alan. You took me by surprise and I'm afraid I behaved very foolishly."

Alan looked at her in consternation. "Foolishly? You behaved the way any normal woman would under the circumstances. I've never known anyone who could cool off so fast. I mean, after being simply wonderful. That's what I've been trying to make you understand. You let yourself go and then almost instantly decide that you've done something very unwise. Why? It isn't natural for a woman to feel that way."

A slight flush crept up over her face and she looked at him almost angrily. "You're very sure of yourself, aren't you?"

"What do you mean?"

"You seem to know all about how a woman should feel when you kiss her. You must have kissed a great many women, Alan. You've let your success go to your head."

"Have I? I don't think so. Of course I've kissed a great many women. I've never known one to behave the way you do. I can't understand you at all. Do you like to be kissed or don't you? If it gives you pleasure there's no reason in the world for you to draw back like that. If you're afraid of what it might lead to you're just being foolish. You don't have to be afraid. We're adult human beings—at least I hope we are. I think I have a fair measure of control. I believe you have. You'd think I'd asked you to sleep with me."

"Alan!"

"I'm sorry if my candor shocks you. You shock very

easily—and I'm sorry and I wish you didn't. You know damned well I want to marry you. How many times have I asked you? I've lost count, and I'm not too good at simple mathematics anyway. Even Einstein wasn't."

"Alan, I'd rather not talk about it. At least, not right now."

"I'm sorry," Alan said. "I didn't mean to upset you. But that quality of emotional out-going I've been talking about is very important to me in a woman. Not all men may feel that way, but I do. An unresponsive woman has nothing to give me. A woman can deeply love a man and remain unresponsive in a physical way. It's possible—theoretically, at least. To some men it may not matter too much. They may even prefer to do all the love making themselves.

"But to me—that's primitive. It just isn't mature. It may well have been the pattern followed by our primitive ancestors for five hundred thousand years. Women were taken captive in war. They were not free and independent and didn't really have the right to make love. They were made love to. The captive bird, the hypnotized rabbit. Often the cruelly crushed bird or rabbit. And there's something in the male animal that finds a fierce pleasure in that, if he's primitive enough. And if a woman is sufficiently primitive she may find pleasure in it too.

"All right. Say that all men have a little of that primitiveness in them. Perhaps they should have a little of it, or they fail as lovers. But if it becomes a dominant impulse in lovemaking you sink to the level of the jungle again.

"It isn't the creative way. It doesn't enrich the human personality as it should be enriched by sex—by an out-going of love and tenderness on the part of both partners. It isn't enough just to make love. You have to feel that you are loved in return. It might be better to be loved in return by even a physically unresponsive woman than not to be loved at all.

"In fact, it would be better. Why do men make such complete romantic fools of themselves over just one woman? Often she doesn't begin to be as physically attractive as a dozen 'easy' girls they could pick up at random. But what they are searching for is something very precious and unique—a deep capacity to love them in return.

"Even that can become morbid, almost an obsession. A man can make a complete fool of himself in an effort to please the woman, can cater to her slightest whim. You might be able to do that to me. I don't know, I'm not sure. But it's because I feel myself to be so vulnerable that I'm talking to you like this."

For a moment Ann didn't say anything at all. She just stood quietly staring at him, and there was a look on her face that he could not remember ever having seen before.

He suddenly realized that she was no longer angry, that in some wholly inexplicable way his words had dissolved at least one of the barriers between them, and drawn her closer to him. Even before she drew closer to him physically her sudden change of mood made itself felt like a tangible presence in the room—an aura of warmth and forgiveness radiating out from her.

She was coming toward him now and he sat very still, telling himself that he had only to wait for the forgiveness to become complete. He waited and almost before he knew what had happened she was lying snugly against him on the sofa, her head cradled on his shoulder.

He knew that he could have kissed her then and she would not have drawn back. But he did not kiss her. Instead he took one of her hands and caressed it gently.

"You create too many problems for yourself, darling," she said. "Sometimes I think you're absolutely crazy to torment yourself the way you do—with your strange insistence on analyzing everything. You should live more from moment to moment. A moment like this, for instance, is very precious. Why must you look ahead so much—or back so much?"

"I don't know why," Alan said. "I guess I'm just made that way."

"Of course, the Screep's terribly important to you. You don't like to see men die. You were torn apart, so you came here to tell me about it. You were bitter and angry. You felt helpless and alone. Don't you suppose I knew what you were going through?"

"I thought perhaps you did know. But I couldn't be sure. Do you mind if I talk a little more about it?"

"Of course not, darling. I shouldn't have interrupted you before. But the dinner was getting cold. When a woman has prepared a dinner for the man she loves and it doesn't turn out right she can be torn up too."

"Sure, I understand. I'm sorry. I didn't mean to—"

"Never mind that now, darling. Tell me more about the Screep. It concerns me too. I know it's selfish of me, but I do want to stay alive—if only to go on loving you. If too many of our ships are shot down there won't be any more small white cottages, or plumbers' bills or cribs with babies in them or even a starling hopping about in the rain. There'll just be blood on shattered floors beneath dead men and women, and skeleton window frames."

"No," Alan said. "It will be more final than that. Like a figured bowl that has been sandblasted inside and out. The figures will be gone and the bowl will shine with its own light. It takes a long time for radioactivity to die out."

"So we mustn't let that happen."

"We can't let it happen. I don't even want to think that it could happen."

"You say our ships aren't piloted by the right kind of men.

Aren't men who are willing to die to enable the rest of us to go on living the right kind, Alan? Won't we win in the end just because there are such men in the world—a great many such men?"

"I'm afraid not. I know what you're trying to say. You're trying to say that the human spirit at its most courageous can never go down to utter defeat. If it's defeated once it will rise and walk again. But you've got to be realistic about that. Life is always a struggle and if you take it for granted that you'll win that struggle anyway—you may not win it at all.

"I've said that our pilots are better trained than the Enemy's, and they are. I'm simply stating a fact. I've said that our radar is two hundred miles better than theirs, and it is. Another fact. But our men are dying faster than we can replace them. And the Enemy's men are not. The Enemy stays very much alive.

"With odds like that are you still convinced we'll win in the end?"

"But you said—a different type of trainee. Some kind of psychotic. I thought sanity was the surest guarantee of survival in any struggle."

"Ordinarily it would be. But we're up against something monstrous and abnormal. Something that has all of our best sane minds baffled completely. Understand me, Ann. I'm groping in a very terrible kind of darkness. We've got to do something with the Screep to keep fear at bay. Monstrous, paralyzing, killing fear.

"When a child wakes up at night in a darkened room and starts screaming his mother can sometimes soothe and quiet him with a few reassuring words. But not always. Sometimes he'll go right on screaming and become so terrified she'll have to send for the family physician—a kindly man who may or may not know what to do. He may have to use very unorthodox methods.

"We're babes in the woods here, Ann. We're not so much the physician as the screaming child itself. Maybe the doctor will try to get the child to help himself, save himself. The doctor and the screaming child will be fused together in a kind of super-personality—half child, half wise man. Such a personality may appear to function psychotically. But it may also have a very good chance of succeeding."

"I'm not sure I should have asked you to talk about it, Alan. You'll have to think about it again tomorrow and talking about it now may not do you any good at all. Perhaps we should go back to talking about how to persuade me to love you in the right way."

She moved closer to him and for a moment he couldn't quite fathom the expression in her eyes. He was struck by guilt, because he knew that he had been more than a little unfair to her. He decided to repeat the words she had said to him.

"You create too many problems for yourself, sweetheart," he said. "You should live more from moment to moment. Didn't Walter Pater say something like that once? About living for the moment with a hard, gem-like flame? Only— let's not make the flame too hard and gem-like."

CHAPTER SIX

GARVEY AND HIS companions left the theater and moved casually across a broad, elm-shaded avenue toward the Common. Garvey and Tabor walked abreast and Freddy lagged some thirty paces behind. There was stark fear in Wills' eyes and his steps dragged a little. He seemed to be in no hurry to catch up with death wearing only the thinnest of disguises.

There was a cool breeze blowing across the Common and it would have been a nice evening if it hadn't been for the War. The War spoiled the evening for almost everyone, but it was spoiled in an exciting way as far as Garvey and Tabor were concerned.

They paused for an instant to listen to a stump speaker who was apparently a little cracked. The War had made a lot of people either wildly neurotic or mildly psychotic and the stump speaker belonged in the second category.

The stump speaker was saying: "It's really very simple when you analyze it. You hear a lot of talk about science leaping so far ahead of human wisdom and human morality that there's no possible way of preventing War. But let's take a sober second look at what science has accomplished. All over the world medical science has advanced in seven-league boots. People seldom die young anymore—if you write off the accident toll and the War toll.

"We've conquered disease in a three-way victory. Antibiotics cure or control every bacteriological or virus-carried disease in medical literature. Old age has been retarded by an incredible advance in gerontal knowledge. We know exactly what causes aging and how to slow up the process. And diet—good diet has done more to increase the health of the under-privileged than decent sanitation. But both have played their parts. A three-way victory. A glorious victory.

"Or take industrialization. Science has enabled us to build machines that have completely eliminated machine-operating drudgery for two billion men and women in every corner of the world. The average workday even in Indonesia is now five hours. And atomic fission has made the world's dwindling natural fuel supply of no consequence whatever. We don't need oil or coal—we have harnessed the wild stallions at the core of exploding suns.

"The tortured human being himself? Modem psychology has at its disposal techniques that should completely eliminate that torture. Were it not for the tension and the horror of War there would be no psychotics. Poverty? Yes, yes—we have a little of it left. The under-privileged are still with us. But we are making tremendous strides toward eliminating slums and poverty and in another twenty years—

"But I am straying from the main point—the point which I'm convinced must be made forcibly now if it is to be made at all. It must be hammered home, so to speak, and I intend to do so with all the gifts of eloquence at my command.

"Why do we all live in constant fear? Why does War threaten our very existence and the existence of our children's children?

"I'll tell you why. The airplane. First the airplane and then spaceships, space stations, space flight. Just think for a moment. If the airplane had never been invented all of the great advances of modern science could have been used for the exclusive benefit of mankind! Think, think, think. If we still rode on horseback or traveled in coaches—or even if we traveled solely in buses and express trains and ocean liners and did not possess the airplane, the spaceship?

"Man is unstable, you see. He is like a radioactive isotope.

He is magnificent if something he is powerless to control with his mind does not trigger him to a sudden, world-destroying explosiveness. Air travel is hyper-dimensional. It enables a man to get immediately over and above the people or the social structures he would like to see erased.

"It's a quick, sure, terrifying way of *striking* back. Of striking out hard without carefully weighing of all the issues at stake—without any psychological planning or meditation or the kind of wisdom-sense that dominated the thinking of the ancient Greeks. No vessel of human intelligence as volatile as the human organism should have been exposed to such a temptation."

"I think he's got something there," Taber said.

"It's all Greek to me," replied Garvey. "Maybe he's got a grudge against the guy who first invented airplanes. Who was it?"

"A guy named Wright, you dope."

"Then this Wright guy was a wrong guy, if you ask me."

"I'm not asking you. But why don't you ask him?"

"All right, I will…hey, Buster! Who invented the airplane? Me and my friend here would like to know."

The stump speaker stopped talking abruptly. He fixed Garvey with an irate stare, his lips setting into tight, resentful lines. He was a small, wiry man with a great shock of red hair that bulged out on both sides of his head.

"I don't like to be interrupted by young hoodlums," he said, his voice forceful. "But just to keep the record straight I'll tell you. His name was Curtis."

"Yeah. Is that really so, Buster? My buddy here claims it was a guy named Wright."

"Young man, the matter has been in dispute for well over a century. But no good purpose would be served by discussing it with you. The man who invented the airplane is criminally responsible for the plight of the world today. But

I'm quite sure that the meaning of 'criminal responsibility' would completely elude you. Your ignorance is too abysmal."

"You lousy crackpot!" Garvey said, a dark flush creeping up over his cheekbones. "Who do you think you're insulting?"

"That's a strange word for you to use, young man. You cannot insult a person without human dignity or respect for his elders. No, I'll be fair. Not all elders deserve respect. I should have said that you can't insult a person who does not even know the meaning of personal integrity and has no reason to care what anyone else may think of him."

"Fancy-pants words. You're going to take them back."

The knife came out, snapped open. Garvey advanced on the stump speaker with the blade half-concealed by his palm and his shoulders quivering in enraged bull fashion.

The stump speaker's audience scattered. It was a very small audience—an audience with no strong convictions in regard to the speaker and hence with no capacity for martyrdom. The one woman gasped in horror and retreated backwards across the pavements. The seven men simply turned and walked away quickly.

Had the men realized that the speaker was tragically and hopelessly insane they might have stayed to defend him, if only out of compassion. But his psychosis was an unusual one. It had swept away his emotional stability but he still retained sufficient residual contact with reality to enable him to talk glibly and with erudition. Indeed, there was considerable truth and logic in his contentions, and only a first-rate mind could have demonstrated that he was the kind of lunatic who could ride a monomania with an outward display of almost absolute normalcy.

You can fool most of the people a good part of the time with that kind of psychosis, and Garvey remained completely unaware that the stump speaker's curse of the airplane was a psychotic fantasy.

Garvey could not have said exactly *why* the man was a crackpot. He only knew that the poor devil's mind was *wide open*. It was vulnerable, it was full of squirmy worms of fear and false hopes—call them organically damaged neurons if you're so inclined—and the man himself was so locked in a death grapple on the shifting sands of unreason that Garvey could with savage joy think of him as a *perfect victim*.

A physically weak man has much to fear from primitive human brutality. His only recourse is to the Law, and the Law is seldom on hand to assist him when his need of protection becomes urgent. A mentally unstable man is in an even worse predicament. If he summons the Law he may find himself facing not a rescuer, but a remorseless and misguided accuser.

Garvey knew this only too well. Advancing on the speaker with his knife in readiness he hardly gave a thought to possible police interference.

In this case, he felt, it wasn't necessary. If the cops saw what was going on and rushed in to interfere he, Garvey, would become a law-abiding citizen. He'd simply point to the speaker and say: *He's ticky in the coco. Just look at him! Look at the way he's jerking his shoulders around, listen to what he's saying. If you had a sister would you want her to stand here and listen to talk like that? Sure, sure, he's starting to clam now. But before you got here you should have heard him. And there was a woman right here and when I saw what was going on I knew I'd have to do something.*

"Keep away from me!" the stump speaker warned. "I'll summon the police. I'm not afraid of you. That knife doesn't frighten me."

"It doesn't, eh?" Garvey said, winking at Tabor. He grabbed the speaker by his coat lapels, precisely as he had grabbed Wills, and let the blade of the knife rest coldly for an instant against his victim's right cheek.

"Oh, gawd!" the little man croaked under his breath.

"Now then," Garvey said. "Take it back. Talk it all back slowly and carefully."

"What do you mean? What do you want me to say?"

"You said I was ignorant. Do you still believe that?"

"No, I—Oh, damn you, yes! I do mean it. You're ignorant and brutal and vicious."

Garvey's eyes seemed to change color. Always dark, they became ink-black, opaque. "You don't want to go on living, is that it?"

The little man remained silent, his eyes on Garvey's face. He seemed hardly to hear what Garvey was saying. Possibly he did hear but the knife was inching so swiftly toward his jugular that he could hardly have been blamed for keeping his mouth shut.

"Well, Buster? Do you take it back, or do I take it from here?"

"Here comes a cop!" Tabor warned suddenly, gripping Garvey's arm. "The creep's got a license to speak. He may not be as crazy as you think."

Garvey released the stump speaker with a curse. He stepped back and snapped the knife shut.

"Quick, put away that shiv!" Tabor warned. "We've got to breeze—and fast."

Garvey hesitated, wondering if he should brazen it out. Give the lousy crackpot something to worry about—a night at least in the clink. He'd been prepared to force a showdown right in the presence of the cops. Was he turning chicken?

No, that wasn't it. But a guy had to go through with his plans, when once he had something big worked out for kicks. The crackpot wasn't important. He'd thrown a scare into him and watched him turn white—so what more was there to do? He'd had no real intention of finishing the windy creep

47

off. First-degree homicide could get a guy in deep and keep him breathing in prison smells for a third of his life.

Garvey turned and saw that Freddy Wills had crept up like a jelly mouse, and was waiting for him to take off. Tabor was waiting too, his face anxious, one eye on the cop.

The stump speaker had seen the cop now and was opening his mouth to shout. Garvey inched forward, nodding and smiling, and drove his fist into the crackpot's stomach, hard. The little man groaned and sank to the pavement like a lump of lard dropped on a skillet by a chef with no time to waste.

"Okay, here we go!" Garvey said. "Don't run—just keep walking away fast."

They walked away fast. They headed for the Common in a direction that was somewhat roundabout, keeping to the shadows of the big elms and pausing only once to light cigarettes and wolf-eye a passing blonde.

There were six big recruiting trucks lined up on the Common, a hundred feet apart. It was just a question of choosing the right one—the one least likely to explode. But since there was no way of telling from the outside how alert—or careless—the guards might be inside, the problem really boiled down to picking a truck with no bomb display on its rear platform.

There were two such trucks and Garvey picked the nearest one.

"Here's how we'll work it," he said. "We're just three guys who can hardly wait to enlist, see? We'll let the sergeant come out on the platform, give us a quick up-and-down and start talking. Then we'll go up the ramp while he's getting his hook straightened out, bait and all. I'll rock him with a hard right just as you go past—or maybe I'll smack him first across the mouth to keep him from yelling out. Then I'll topple him down the ramp to the pavement. By then you two should be inside the truck.

"Inside there may be two or three guards. We each take care of one. We don't let it turn into a general scrap—just one guard apiece. If I have to use the shiv—okay, I'll use it. But I don't want to use it. Any questions?"

"No questions, kid," Tabor said.

"Okay, then. Why are we standing here?"

Garvey started walking toward the truck, assuming an easy, nonchalant air, a cigarette dangling from his lips. Tabor walked almost at his elbow and Freddy Wills trailed by a scant seven feet.

They reached the truck's tail lights and paused directly in front of the ramp, staring up to where it broadened out into a circular platform.

Almost instantly a recruiting sergeant emerged from the darkness overhead and stood staring down at them, his genial face illumed by the glow of the streetlights on the Common.

"I take it you lads are just drifting around sight-seeing," he said. "Maybe you'd like to stop drifting for a minute or two and come inside for a cup of coffee!"

Tabor nudged Garvey's elbow. "That's a new pitch," he whispered. "They get you drugged with caffeine and up you go into space."

"Pipe down," Garvey cautioned. "Let him talk. If he invites us inside a second time we'll take him up on it."

"Why not right now?"

"Shut up—quiet. I want to size him up first. He's a husky looking bastard."

"How about it, men? We've got some War trophies inside you might like to look over. We've got a propeller that came off an Enemy TU 99 that was launched from a twenty-jet mother ship in low flight over Texas. They could have bombed out three cities but our men got them first. We've got a flare bomb that could light up every state in the Union. We've got a little helium bomb of our own—all triggered and ready. You set it off with acid that eats its way right down to where it's radioactively unstable."

"That sure is interesting," Garvey said. "The Enemy must have done a lot of sweating."

"You bet it's interesting. Any young fellow who could look at some of the things we've got inside here and wait around to be drafted ain't my idea of a man. We like fine, bright, multi-stage installations—don't we, boys? Just to run your hands over them makes you feel proud to be a part of what's going on. It's bigger than we are—a tribute to the resourcefulness of the men in the big-bomber labs. We'd trade it all in for a sure, lasting peace, but we can't wait around for peace to come—not when the Enemy is right upstairs. Come inside, men."

"We're coming," Garvey said. He tossed his cigarette away. "Go up easy and quiet," he whispered, patting Tabor on the arm. "Don't let Freddy get ahead of you. If he goes inside first he'll mess everything up. We want to get a good feeling out of this."

"I'll watch it. Let's go."

Garvey walked slowly up the ramp, a broad grin on his face. "You been upstairs much yourself, sergeant?" he asked.

"You bet I have. High cabin temperatures sent me to the hospital five times. But I'm back on the job, as you can see. I go up again tomorrow."

"Maybe so, sergeant," Garvey said. "But tonight you go down for a lousy count of ten."

Garvey didn't adhere to his original plan. He hit the sergeant three times. The first blow caught him in the pit of the stomach and doubled him up. The second was a hammer-blow to the small of his back just above the kidney, as he lurched forward and the third was a savage repeat which sent him spinning down the ramp.

He twisted sideways an instant before he hit the pavement and rolled over twice. He didn't move after that—just lay sprawled out like a heavy grain sack that had met with an unloading foul-up and was waiting for a lifting crane to straighten it out.

Garvey's eyes were very bright. So far, everything was working out. He stepped back and let Tabor go in first. But when Freddy's white, frightened face came close he pushed him back and whispered fiercely: "You look scared as hell. Keep behind me, and pick the smallest guy. Use your knuckles. When you get him down bang his head against the floor."

The advice proved unnecessary. There was only *one* guard inside and Tabor had moved into his neighborhood so fast and brutally that he was flat on his back when Garvey and Willis came into view. Tabor was bending over him, half-dragging, half-pushing him toward the door.

Garvey seemed disappointed. "Only one hopped-up soldier to guard a truck like this? Who'd have believed it?"

"He nearly got me," Tabor wheezed. "He came at me with a wrench. Come on, give me a hand with him."

"Okay. We'll toss him out after the sergeant."

Garvey bent and grabbed the guard by the neckband of his dun-colored service jacket. In a moment they had him out through the door and were rolling him down the ramp.

It was just like tossing a second sack after the first.

Tabor was breathing heavily when they went back inside, but Garvey remained poised and cool.

"First we've got to get that ramp up," he said. "There's the switch—see it? 'Ramp Release' in big red letters. Go on, throw it and see what happens."

"Maybe it won't raise the ramp," Freddy said, his face drained of all color. "Maybe it's just to let the ramp down."

"What the hell! Come on, get over there and reverse it. That's all you have to do."

Freddy obeyed. He crossed to the switch and threw it to dead center. There was a loud, churning sound. The truck began to vibrate. Garvey walked out on the back platform and stared down. His face remained calm.

"It's going up, all right!" he called back. "No cops in sight. The soldier boys aren't moving."

"Come back in here and help us!" Tabor shouted. "I'm not sure I know how to drive this heap!"

"Sure, I'll be right there. Keep your shirt on."

Drive right down the Common and then open up. We keep going and maybe circle the freight yards and come straight back. We bust speed records getting back. We show 'em we're not afraid to come back. Maybe we don't pick up a dame tonight. Maybe we do. There's kicks in this even if we don't pick up a dame. We'll show 'em we never punk out.

"Hey, what's keeping you? You want to have the whole United States army on our necks?" Garvey cried.

The ramp was almost up now. With a creaking and a rasping it slid into grooved bearings high up under the platform.

Garvey lit a cigarette, very slowly and deliberately. Then he went back inside.

"Okay, everybody," he said. "Now we can get started."

CHAPTER SEVEN

ANN HAD TURNED the phono-vision on. Alan was staring at her shapely legs as she sat on the sofa opposite him, but for the moment, at least, it was a purely clinical scrutiny. He'd read somewhere that European males did not particularly go for trim feminine ankles. They liked them, of course, but there was no fetish adoration involved, no particular concentration on that particular aspect of femininity. American males did go for shapely ankles—in a big way. Why? It was a little difficult to understand.

"What are you thinking about, darling?" Ann asked, between a PV commercial and the blank space that followed after it.

Alan started to tell her and then decided against it. You couldn't come right out and say to a woman: "I was thinking about your ankles," and not expect her to get angry.

That was the ironic part of it. Here he was thinking thoughts that any woman would have been overjoyed to have spelled out for her in big, shining letters. And he couldn't even start off with those few simple words, *I was thinking about your ankles. Nothing else about you is quite so important to me.*

"You must be thinking about *something*? What is it, darling? The Screep again? Can't you get it off your mind for just this one night? How would I feel being married to a man who wakes up in the middle of the night and says: 'I'm terribly worried about the Screep. Maybe I should get up and get dressed and go back to the station. Maybe the Screep needs me. Or maybe I need the Screep. You don't mind, do you, honeybunch? I'll be back early and we can have breakfast together.' "

"It could happen, of course," Alan admitted ruefully.

"But the War won't last forever."

"I sometimes wonder."

He was spared the embarrassment of a reply by a sudden interruption of the commercial. It was not just a blank space this time. It was an emergency, police-military, news flash, and it came in loud and glaring.

"We interrupt this program to bring you a War Office Emergency Announcement. A recruiting truck has just been seized by three unidentified men on Boston Common. The truck has left the Common and is heading north. The men are young—possibly teen-age delinquents. But we have no positive assurance that they are not Enemy spies intent on sabotage.

"We repeat. We have no positive assurance that the men are ordinary criminals. The truck contains two small atomic warheads. The warheads have not been activated, but there are solid rocket propellants in the truck would could be used to blow up military installations anywhere in the city. If the men are technicians with a specialized knowledge of nuclear weapons there are materials in the truck that could easily be used to activate the warheads.

"The Common must be cleared of all traffic immediately. It will be used by the police and the militia as a base for pursuit operations. Aerial and ground pursuit installations are now being set up at both ends of the Common. All pedestrians and all vehicles must leave the Common. Repeat—all civilian vehicles must leave immediately.

"The truck is now being traced by radar. In a moment we will have more definite information. Until pursuit planes are in the air the danger will continue grave. We urge that you stay tuned to this station."

Alan groaned. "Until pursuit planes are in the air," he said, striding across the room to move the brightness and contrast dials forward. "This should be a *ground pursuit* job all the way. Forty or fifty years ago they would have handled it better. That's progress for you—with cleated shoes. Forty years ago there were police cars at every intersection. The instant a short-wave alert went out they started converging on the lawbreaker from a dozen directions."

"But there are atomic bombs in that truck," Anne protested. "I should think aerial pursuit would be absolutely necessary."

"What can a plane do?" Alan demanded. "Drop an even bigger bomb? It's making a mountain out of a very deadly kind of molehill."

His lips tightened. "Everything could go. Bunker Hill, Paul Revere, the Old North Church. Emerson, Hawthorne, Lowell. Two centuries of Harvard, Beacon and Chestnut Hills. The Lodges speak only to the Cabots and the Cabots speak only to God. Even that kind of snobbery would be better than no Boston at all. Everything could go—and all because some maniac in the War Office puts live atomics in a recruiting truck!"

"But the bombs can't be activated. At least, not easily."

"Can't they? Inside that truck are little phials of acid. You pour the acid into a pin-sized hole in the warhead and it eats its way to the fission mechanism in precisely thirty-two seconds."

"Phials of acid? I don't believe it."

"Why not? Everything must be genuine—the real McCoy. They've been using live ammunition in war training maneuvers for a century and a half. Why not also to stimulate recruiting? Do you want recruiting to fall off? Of course you don't. You'd rather have—no Boston."

Alan spoke with the bitterness of a man so completely in the grip of unreason that he had half-succeeded in convincing himself there might be only a few more minutes left in the world to talk at all.

"Let a man run his fingers over the real McCoy, let him be convinced that just by a flick of the wrist he could destroy a city—and he'll want to make sure that the Enemy doesn't get a chance to destroy *his* city. The feel of death right under your thumb. There's nothing like it to stimulate recruiting— or so the War Office claims. They could just as easily fill those phials with water.

"But someone just might find out, someone might carry tales. Besides, it's the honorable way. Lies are for the Enemy. Rather than do anything that smacks even remotely of deception, the War Office would rather have no Boston. It's a beautiful kind of idealism. But sometimes I think that sober, realistic thinking departed from the human race long before the first Neanderthaler cracked a skull."

"I still don't believe there are phials of acid in that truck," Ann said with stubborn conviction.

"Neither do I," Alan conceded grudgingly. "But there might just as well be. I was merely using that as an illustration. There are other ways of activating an atomic warhead. And you don't always have to be an expert—if the trigger mechanism is nine-tenths in place. A little carelessness, a lurch against a side rail and—no Boston. Naturally they wouldn't tell you that in an emergency broadcast designed for public consumption. It might alarm the ladies. There'd be a knitting circle outcry and the War Office would be in trouble."

Alan shook his head in anger, his close-cut hair catching highlights from the screen. "It would be one case where a knitting circle outcry would be justified. I can give you a much simpler illustration. Just picture Boston as a big, smoking crater—"

He was interrupted by another flash bulletin. An announcer of national prominence appeared on the screen, a cavernous-browed young man with a genius for making the most of spot-coverage assignments.

"Hilton Emery," Ann said. Under ordinary circumstances she would have added, "Oh, I like him!" But the circumstances were hardly ordinary and Emery seemed prepared and determined to make himself disliked, if it should prove necessary.

Emery said: "The War Office has instructed me to warn all unauthorized civilians to stay away from the Common, the shipyards and the city's guided missile installations on Chestnut Hill. Civilians disobeying this warning will be subject to instant arrest and will face very serious charges. I repeat. Unless you are an authorized person or a member of the armed forces on active duty you must stay away from all of these areas.

"Civilians in general are advised to stay indoors, to keep off the streets as much as possible. All commercial traffic has been halted throughout the city. All strollers have been halted. All heli-cabs have been ordered to stay on the ground. No one must enter the underground. Trains will be running, but any civilian who attempts to board a train will be halted and questioned by the military.

"The recruiting truck has been located. It has encircled the Air Research and Air Development Command Center and is heading back toward the Common. There are a good many planes overhead now. Ground crews have been alerted and ten helicoptic jets are about to take off from Simpson Field. Roadblocks have been set up as a precautionary measure on all important intersections north and northwest of the city. A street-by-street security alert system is in full operation throughout the city.

"But for obvious reasons no attempt can be made to halt the truck from the air or by ground intervention until it returns to the Common. Specialized equipment has been set up on the Common for this purpose, and air and ground units have worked out a plan of attack that should have a very good chance of succeeding. The situation is serious, but there is no justification for panic. I repeat. There is absolutely no justification for panic."

"He doesn't believe that for one moment," Alan said.

His voice was matter-of-fact, but there was something in his eyes that made Ann stiffen in concern. She had seen the look before. They were both silent for an instant and she kept hoping that his expression would change. A touch of caution and self-restraint would have changed it, but she realized even before he spoke again that there was no caution in him.

"I'm *not* an unauthorized civilian," he said. "Just by flipping open my wallet and displaying an identification card I can be on the Common when the big show starts."

"Alan, you wouldn't—"

"Why not? I can be there in five minutes. It's just a few blocks. I can make it in a fast walk. No need to drive, and risk having some trigger-happy soldier take a pot-shot at my car before I can wave my card at him."

"No, Alan—please. You can't take such a chance. You'll be walking into an inferno. You—you—"

"Yes?"

Her voice quavered and almost broke. "You must be out of your mind. You must be, to even think of such a thing. You've no right to go—no right to be there at all. You'll just be in the way. If you're killed you'll have only yourself to blame."

"A good many men may be dying tonight," Alan said. "If they have to use just one small atomic projectile to stop that truck—well! I want to be in on it, Ann. I know it's hard for a woman to understand. But I've got to be in on it. I've no choice. The big show is too near—only a few blocks away.

If I stayed here and just let it happen and didn't participate I'd feel rotten about it all the rest of my days."

"You'd feel better in your grave?"

"That's unfair, Ann—and you know it. I'm sorry. Can't you see how it is? I've wasted a full minute, just trying to make you understand. I can't waste another."

He kissed her before he left, but she did not open her lips to receive the kiss and her arms did not go about him.

She watched him go into the entrance hall, put on his hat and glance back at her for an instant with accusing eyes.

Then the door slammed.

She barely hesitated at all. The coldness of the kiss she had given him was like a lump of ice resting on her tongue. It wasn't his kiss that had turned to ice, but her own half-kiss and it lingered with her and its coldness was so great a reproach that she felt like screaming:

"Come back, darling. I didn't mean it. Come back, and I'll kiss you as you've never been kissed before. It may be the last time—the very last time I'll ever kiss you. I don't want you to go to your death thinking I don't love you, thinking I'm cold. Oh, please, darling—just give me one more brief last chance!"

She knew what she'd have to do, of course. She'd have to run. If she was going to follow him and overtake him she'd have to run until she was out of breath and even then she might never see him again. He would walk fast, very fast and he was a man and he had a long stride.

Well, a woman's stride could be long too. A woman with a knife in her heart doesn't have to worry too much about appearing feminine when she runs to bring all of herself to the man she loves. He'll forgive her and overlook it, even if she has to run like a Tomboy.

Out of the door and down the stairs to the street she raced, telling herself that it was too late, that he had already turned the corner, that the night had swallowed him. She had lost him forever and there was no hope now, no light in the darkness, no way of bringing him back.

Then she saw him. She was outside the apartment building now and she saw him heading for the corner and the wide intersection beyond, saw the light on his shoulders as he moved further and further away from her into the night.

She began to run. She might have caught up with him then, but a cab moving south in defiance of the stand-still forced her to halt for an instant in the middle of the intersection and when she broke into a run again he had quickened his stride. She shouted for him to wait, to wait only for a moment, but the night was too loud with competing sound.

Planes roared overhead, and there was a droning everywhere and she could hardly hear herself when she shouted...and she could hardly hear. She ran until she was out of breath and kept on running, but she could not quite catch up with him, for he had begun to run too.

They were very near the Common now. She could see the lights in the sky, crisscrossing, weaving about and the rocket flares and the shouts of the military, and she wanted to die.

It was a man's world and she was not a part of it—no woman like her could ever really be a part of that world. Nurses could be a part of it, and women ambulance drivers and staff officer assistants. But she just wasn't that kind of a woman, she couldn't even stand the sight of blood.

Why couldn't he stop for just one little moment, pause to look around him, pause to look up at the sky? There was death in the sky tonight, terrible with great dark wings unfolding. Death and destruction for three men in a truck.

What were the men in the truck like? In stealing the truck they had behaved like Alan in a way. They had embraced danger as if danger were a woman, terrible and fiery and insatiable in her demands.

Why did danger seem to draw men like a magnet? Why did they always walk toward it instead of away from it, inviting destruction, inviting the thunderbolts?

Not all men. Some men were simple cowards. But those who weren't seemed to embrace danger for its own sake, as if it were a positive good in itself.

She had never thought herself capable of running so fast. She had almost caught up with Alan now and yet there was still a barrier of distance between them that her footsteps could not span.

The Common was in clear view when she saw the truck. It was coming in fast from the right, a banner of light streaming out before it. She knew at once that it was the expected truck, the only truck that could have taken away her life by taking Alan's life.

She stopped running. Alan stopped too, a few feet from a soldier with a half-raised gun. In another moment the soldier would have stepped forward and challenged Alan's right to be there, would have demanded to see his identification card immediately.

But that moment never came. There was a sudden burst of gunfire, and the Common became bright with crisscrossing beams of light and the sky itself seemed to turn to flame.

CHAPTER EIGHT

FREDDY WILLS WAS screaming. He was clinging to a swaying copper rail directly behind Garvey and screaming because he could not keep the fear locked up inside him any longer. It had become so unbearable that he didn't care if Garvey swung about in the driver's seat and put a quick end to his life.

Garvey's face was white. Tabor wasn't saying anything, just swallowing hard as he helped Garvey drive the truck, a man who was still too much of a boy to fully realize what was happening. What was happening would stop the truck before long, and Garvey knew that time was running out on him.

He would have very little chance of escaping from the truck alive. The thought was hateful to him, but he wasn't frightened. That was the strange part of it. He felt good, almost exultant. The truck was under fire and shells were exploding all about it, but even the hateful thought of death did not frighten Garvey. It did not frighten him and even though it was hateful it could not keep him from feeling good.

We've got them scared, he thought. They're afraid of what's inside this truck. The white-livered bastards! They don't dare try to get us with an atomic projectile.

Why was Freddy screaming? To be such a weak sister was one hell of a thing. Any guy who was born that way should be dropped on his head at birth.

He turned suddenly and said: "Stop that, Freddy, or I'll kill you."

Freddy went right on screaming.

Another shell burst outside the truck. It sent a dark line zigzagging across the windshield, but the glass was unbreakable. It could not be shattered.

Tabor muttered. "We should never have come back. Never! We didn't have to do this! I must have been crazy to listen to you!"

"Shut up!" Garvey said. "I'm not sorry we came back. We'll make those brass-shouldered punks bring out the whole army and the air force—just so we can watch the monkeys turn green. Don't take your hand off that brake. But don't slam down on it either, unless I tell you."

"How far can we get? If we stop now they'll stop firing. Do you want to be blown apart?"

"Sure, why not? It would be worth it."

"Kid, you're out of your mind. I should never have listened—"

"You did listen. Don't forget that. We're all in this together. In another second, though, there's goin' to be just two of us. Can't you make that fluff-boy back there shut up?"

"Maybe he has a right to die anyway he wants to," Tabor said.

"I won't die screaming. If they get me in the lungs I'll die wheezing, but not screaming. I'd cut my head off before I'd scream."

"You're not so tough. You're just crazy."

"That's what you think," Garvey said.

Two more shells burst outside the truck. There was a low whining as steel-jacketed bullets hummed past, hundreds of bullets that were accomplishing nothing at all.

"They'll drop a bomb on us if they have to!" Tabor warned, with the huskiness of anguish in his voice. "They'll risk anything to stop us. There must be a hundred planes upstairs. You hear that roar?"

"Let them try," Garvey muttered. "A bomb could miss us and hit them. You think they want to kill ten thousand soldiers?"

Freddy had stopped screaming. There was no longer any breath left in his lungs. He leaned against the rail, making gasping sounds and wishing that he could die.

He was remembering things about himself he wanted to forget. He was remembering the teacher who had said: "Go up and stand in the corner, so that the whole class can see what a sloucher you are. A boy with self-respect doesn't go around slouching, with his hands in his pockets. He doesn't whisper out of the corner of his mouth. Things like that start in the home. Your parents were too indulgent. They've made a sissy out of you."

It hadn't been true at all. His parents had tried to kill him once. First his father had beaten him with a stick and then his mother had come home drunk and beaten him even harder. He'd almost died that time. He'd almost died...

Why was Garvey so different? His father had beaten him too. But he had sassed the old man right back; he had told the old man off right to his face. Why couldn't he hate his father like that? Why was he afraid to hate his father? Why was he afraid not only of his father, but of everybody?

Garvey was cruel and mean, just like his father. So he feared Garvey almost as much as he had feared his father. Now he was going to die...because he feared Garvey. It was terrible; he couldn't stop it from happening.

Garvey turned around then and looked at him. There was hate and loathing in Garvey's eyes, as if by ceasing to scream Freddy had proved himself even more of a coward.

He realized then that Garvey really wanted him to go on screaming. It gave Garvey pleasure to hear him scream and scream and scream. Well, he wasn't going to give Garvey any more pleasure. Let them kill him. He didn't care. It would hurt Garvey more than it would hurt him. There wouldn't be anyone left then for Garvey to torture.

Garvey would be alone then. But I don't want to die, Freddy thought. I'm afraid to die. If another shell explodes I'll start screaming again.

Another shell did explode—another and another. The truck was careening now. But Garvey stopped that by turning back to the wheel, by giving all of his attention to just staying alive.

"We'd better stop!" Tabor moaned. "We haven't killed anybody. It won't be a murder rap. We can walk out with our hands raised and stay alive."

"To them what we've done is worse than murder," Garvey said, his voice harsh with a strange kind of malice. "We're not just holed up in a farmhouse, fighting off the cops. Did you ever hear of treason—high treason? The country's at war. They shoot guys just for going to sleep on guard duty. What do you think they'd do to us?"

"Why did I ever listen to you?"

"Why? For kicks," Garvey said. "I'm the guy who knows how to arrange them. Now shut up—and watch what you're doing."

There was no real need for Tabor to remain alert, for Garvey was now in full control of the truck. And suddenly—the shells stopped exploding.

A silence descended on the Common—a deathly stillness that was like the lull before a storm, the hush that precedes an avalanche. The soldiers had receded into shadows, had ebbed back on both sides of the Common like a tide turned abruptly ghostly, a tide so completely without substance that it was receding without even stirring the seaweed on the rocks.

Even the planes overhead had somehow miraculously succeeded in muffling their jets. Or so it seemed. Probably they hadn't actually—probably there was still a dull roar overhead. Probably the stillness and the silence were partly subjective; a stunned awakening to the absence of shellfire on a broad avenue that had grown unnaturally quiet. There was a contrast, at any rate, between the present stillness and the almost deafening blasts that had been coming at five-second intervals an instant before.

Unfortunately for Garvey there were things about military science that he did not know. In an age when ships moved through the darkness of space far beyond Earth's orbit, nuclear warheads still remained the most powerful destructive weapon known to man.

But there were other weapons. There had to be. Every weapon of war that has been tested against an enemy and has lessened that enemy's striking power can be used in additional striking missions on many fronts and under widely varying circumstances. Tactics change and weapons are altered or modified accordingly. There are small, powerful weapons that have been used only rarely, and have proved of no great value in space. But all weapons have some value, and there are occasions when a rarely used weapon can prove uniquely suited for a particular task.

What Garvey did not know was that when liquid fuel is fed into an engine it must speed up when it passes through a very narrow section of tubing, and will slow down again only when the constriction has been passed. Every physicist is familiar with this flow phenomenon, every hydraulic engineer—but Garvey was neither a physicist nor an engineer.

If by some miracle that narrow tube flow could be further increased it would quickly pass far beyond the speed of sound and eventually the tubing would explode. It would take quite a little time.

Knowing that it would take time, the military had kept the truck under constant shellfire until the important weapon, the ultimate and decisive weapon, could accomplish the mission for which it had been designed.

The speeding-up ray was projected from an instrument that was squat, black, and goggle-eyed, and as it revolved on its turret amidst a powerful fire-support crew of very able men it looked not unlike a midget planetarium projector revealing the marvels of the heavens to an excited group of youngsters.

But of course it was really nothing of the sort. The soldiers on the Common were not youngsters, and if you looked higher you could see that the sky was black with war birds waiting to swoop.

The soldiers on the Common hoped that the planes would not be needed. They were granted their wish, but what happened wasn't in the least spectacular. A few of the soldiers may have been just human enough—just angry and embittered enough—to have rejoiced in the spectacle of an exploding truck, a truck suddenly shattered by a violence both terrible and self-contained—a violence that would make the entire Common quake and yet miraculously fail to spread.

But it just didn't happen that way. The truck simply

slowed down, and came to an abrupt halt. Had the soldiers been inside the truck they might have heard the explosion, but even that is doubtful. A bursting, small, fuel-feed tube makes very little noise.

But if they wished for excitement—for drama and terror—it was not denied them. It was a cruel thing to wish for even when cruel lives were at stake, and perhaps if they had known what was to happen they would have turned away, white and shaken and reviling themselves.

Death striking at random is always a terrible thing to watch—and when it strikes a young boy, human memory is irretrievably seared.

From the back of the truck three youths leapt and raced across the pavement to the shelter of a long row of trees. The trees had wide, spreading branches and the shadows beneath were wide, dark and deep.

But the shadows were not wide enough or deep enough to save the last of the three. He was too slow in leaping from the truck, too slow in running and the machine gun burst struck him just as he reached the tip of the longest shadow—struck him and spun him about.

He sank to the pavement clutching at his chest, a dark wetness welling from his throat, a bewildered, hurt look in his eyes.

It was over in a moment.

Three soldiers converged upon him and one of them bent quickly and covered him with an army blanket. And so Freddy Wills was welcomed into the army at last, and it is quite possible that the knowledge would have pleased him had he been alive and awake and aware of how warm the blanket was, how snugly fitting. He might even have thanked the sergeant for tucking him in so securely. The sergeant had forgotten to blame him, to accuse him, and his eyes were even a little moist and that too might have pleased Freddy

Wills.

Neither the police nor the military could keep the crowds back. They ignored all radio warnings, swarmed from homes and bomb shelters, filled every street and square immediately adjoining the Common and overflowed onto that broad thoroughfare itself. They broke through all protective cordons, mingled with the military and rubbed elbows with the high brass.

And caught in that seething mass of excited men and women were Alan and Ann. They were together again, arm in arm, their bodies touching and at times seeming almost to blend, so grateful were they to be reunited once more.

If there was need for long range ground support, they had it, for the crowd buoyed them up. But it was entirely possible that if they had been alone on the Common they would not have been aware of their aloneness or surrounded by an even denser crowd, would have thought themselves alone.

"If you'd had time to give that soldier your pass what would you have done?" Ann whispered, her fingers tightening on her companion's arm. "Exactly what, darling? I'm curious."

"I'd have been the complete fool you thought me, I guess," Alan said, his much stronger fingers closing very firmly over her hand. "I'd have walked up to General Snodgrass and asked him for a cigarette. 'Hi, General! I'm the guy who's been working on the Screep. You know—to keep ships and pilots from being blown apart in space. Everyone knows me. It's a top-priority job, very important. I'm a big shot, just like you, General. I understand you boys have been having a little trouble here tonight. Anything I can do to help?' "

Ann laughed and snuggled closer to him. "I bet you would, at that. It's probably just about what you'd have said."

"Darling, is that fair? I joke about something, and you throw it up to me."

"I'm not sure we should joke at all," Ann said, her eyes suddenly shadowed. "We're letting ourselves forget they got only one of the men who made off with that truck. The other two escaped. And the one they shot down wasn't really a man at all—just a boy in his late teens. I'm glad it happened further down the Common. I'm glad I didn't have to see it."

"So am I," Alan said. "But you've got to remember that those men—or boys—did something pretty terrible. Even a boy in his teens knows what an atomic explosion can do to a city. I lean backwards in the way I feel about juvenile delinquency. I don't believe that we need harsher enforcement of the law—harsher punishments of any sort. We need far more sympathy and understanding.

"I don't let the sadistic professional moralists fool me— not for a moment. We have to stretch out a helping hand. If we get kicked in the teeth now and then it can't be helped. Every daring social experiment is a risk, as I've told you. But there are a few limits—" Alan let the words trail off.

"But he was just a frightened boy. To machine-gun him down—"

"That was a tragedy. It shouldn't have happened. But those soldiers had no way of knowing he wasn't an Enemy spy. They were under strict orders to shoot to kill, the instant anyone leapt out of that truck and tried to escape. In all good conscience, you can hardly blame them."

"No, I suppose not, Alan. But it seems—horrible."

"Life can be horrible for anyone at times—the innocent as well as the guilty. The innocent are more often than not harder hit than the guilty. Scoundrels make out very well in all walks of life, although we're not supposed to think so."

To lighten Ann's mood Alan said ruminatively. "I

sometimes think I have a little of the scoundrel in me. Perhaps that's why I don't do too badly."

Ann started to smile, but something stopped her. She didn't know what it was at first—it was just an uneasy feeling, a chill premonition that she was being watched by someone.

Then she saw the white, haggard-eyed face in the weaving crowd, the eyes trained directly upon her, the lips moving soundlessly. It was just one face in a wall of faces, but it stood out from all the others.

It was the face of a young man—possibly only two or three years older than the boy she had just been talking about. She thought she recognized the face, but she couldn't be sure for a moment.

Then she was sure and a perhaps not wholly justifiable feeling of panic came upon her.

He was looking at her now with eyes that seemed to undress her as he stared, that made her want to turn away quickly, lest she do something foolish. She would have liked to strike out at him, to slap his face in anger. What right had he to look at her like that? He was a beast and she was quite sure that he knew it.

It wasn't the first time he had looked at her like that, but it was the first time he had dared to do it quite so openly. There was an added contemptuous something in his eyes now that made his stare twice as insulting—an assurance that had been lacking when she had seen him watching her on the corner outside the Propulsion Fuels Building.

His look seemed to say: *I can wait as long as you can, sister. I'm in no hurry.*

And it was true, although she had no way of knowing what Francis Garvey was thinking. There's no hurry, he told himself. A few weeks may go by before my chance comes. I'll wait all winter if I have to. A chance will come. It's got to come. I want her.

Suddenly the face was gone.

Ann pressed closer to Alan, shivering a little. "Take me home, darling," she whispered.

CHAPTER NINE

THE GREY BOSTON winter finally surrendered to the onrush of spring. Eight-oared shells chased the last ice off the Charles. Boys and girls from a dozen schools walked and sprawled on the deepening green of the riverbanks as the sunsets grew friendlier.

And Dr. Alan Kerr worked. He began to remember the ten and twelve hour days when Screep training was his only concern, as a dimly recalled vacation.

There was no let-up in Screep training. If anything, the program was intensified, for the drain on crews was greater than ever. And on top of this was superimposed a crash research program. Alan's week was split down the middle. Three days for training; three days for research; Sundays for conferences, and sleep when he could get it.

The finest instruments they could devise detected nothing but radar coming from the enemy ships. Flickering and pulsating oddly, and frighteningly powerful with new advances in range, but still only radar.

In laboratories all over the country, engineers argued, wore out slip-sticks, drank oceans of coffee, and swore. Computers grew cranky. Rocket men worked to make the ships a little lighter; redesigned nozzles, looking for a little more range; redesigned controls, searching for a way to lift some of the dreadful burden of that intricate, all-or-nothing combat pass; fought for another hundred miles of radar range, and yet another hundred miles.

Careful questioning confirmed the dying pilot's note. The crews admitted they were making their passes in almost uncontrollable terror, which increased as they neared their target, and increased cumulatively from mission to mission.

But they took their ships out gamely, and went back for more.

And the decontamination squad was kept busy and more burial services were read.

The men in Human Resources tried vainly to find a way to fit a Screep into the functional compactness of a fighting ship, hoping to pick up a fragment of useful information. They combed the combat records, looking for the set of ratings that would give a crew the best chance.

Trainee types were refused that had never been refused before. Types were tried that had never been tried before. And gloom hung heavy over them all. They knew that at the very best, their work was only a stopgap—to hold the line till the real answer could be found.

An answer they probably didn't have the time to find.

The team working on the basic problem—Dr. Alan Kerr's team—carried the heaviest burden of all. Though he worked at the heart of an all-encompassing security system, he felt the whole country was looking over his shoulder. Psych men and electronic men worked in teams, trying to solve the riddle of the direct transmission of emotion—trying to throwaway the ultrasonic link, the Resonator they had been so proud of. Now fear—deadly, and growing worse day by day—often took the place of pride.

In laboratories that had always run smoothly and informally, the words 'slave driver,' and 'glory grabber' were heard. Tempers grew frayed. Lifetime friends snapped at each other. Planning conferences exploded into bitterness between navy and scientists that would leave scars for years to come. And always, beyond the immediate bitterness and the frayed nerves, loomed the specter of dying men.

Spring wore into summer. The Charles river filled with boats, the sounds of happy youngsters and worried mothers. In the evenings, music from the esplanade drifted softly against the windows where Alan and his team worked. They were working with two Screeps, trying to convert ultrasonics back to electronic waves duplicating the original neural currents.

They did it, but it didn't work, as it had failed to work before. The electronic waves did not stimulate the corresponding emotions. There was something missing, and they wrestled with the problem day after day, knowing that it contained the answer they were seeking.

A steady flow of improvements finally slowed the climb of the casualty figures. In August they lost twenty-five ships to get seventeen. General Staff went over the production figures, loss ratios, intelligence reports, and decided that with a three-for-two loss ratio they could just barely hold for a year.

Where there had been only the darkest despair, hope began to grow again. A few of the more optimistic research men decided the worst was past. Others, including Alan, felt the situation was a little early for anything but finger crossing.

Their darkest fears were confirmed in September—Black September—when they lost fifty-three crews and forty-two ships. The figures were top secret, but losses like that couldn't be kept secret. And as their horrifying import sank in, a black depression settled over the labs.

Productive work slowed almost to a stop. The researchers went through the motions, doing the best they could. But the spirit, the teamwork, the hope of success had been broken. There just wasn't enough time.

In the United Nations, Teleman, leading Enemy spokesman, displayed a new and ominous affability as he announced that his confederation was considering the construction of a station on the moon for the purpose of conducting studies in astronomy, earth meteorology, and lunar geology.

For a period of about two weeks, depression continued to deepen over the labs. A few of the researchers got drunk, threw wild parties, made reckless love, in apartments that had held all-night bull sessions. Then, as the shock began to lift, the programs slowly got under way again.

It was during this period that Alan called Ann Fitzgerald for the first time in days. Her mood lightened the instant she heard his voice. She'd been feeling profoundly depressed, caught in the contagious gloom of the news reports. Although the teletypes were not carrying the casualty figures, there were somber references to the impending end of the War, which told the story clearly enough.

There was a bantering relief in Ann's greeting. "Where have you been, you louse? I'll bet you've been taking out every blonde in Boston."

He grinned. "How did you guess? I've been taking them down to Havana, three at a time. Your turn's next. But meanwhile, how about dinner and a show with me this evening?"

"Darling, this is so sudden. Will you meet me at that bench near the Swan Boat—the one we sat on with wet paint, the first time you took me out? Then we could go over to Locke-Ober's for chow."

"What time?"

"Eight." She pursed her lips at him. "And wear a carnation in your left lapel, so I can recognize you."

He took a long lazy shower, mixed himself a tall scotch, and read a magazine for an hour. The editor was getting a bit crotchety lately. Still talking about learning to handle ourselves as well as we handle our environment, but he was beginning to sound discouraged. Couldn't blame him for being upset when they'd had to forbid all depressing plots. The story wasn't bad—about an Enemy pilot who did everything wrong.

Then he fell asleep. When he awoke, he was more relaxed than he could remember. He dressed slowly, savoring the thought of seeing Ann, wondering what she'd wear, remembering the graceful way her body moved as she walked—dignified, yet so model glamorous.

There were very few people on the belts, crossing the bridge. He stayed on the slow belt to enjoy the view of the river. One of those long golden October sunsets had placed a halo over the whole city. With time to kill, he sauntered over to Beacon Street, and then slowly down toward the Common, basking in a quite novel feeling of freedom from the grind.

It was surprising how the problems that had seemed so desperate had lost their terror. Things still looked almost hopeless, but they'd probably work out. People had been saying for thousands of years that "if we don't win this war, civilization is done."

And civilization, such as we have, still struggles along. Maybe this will be just another war. Maybe there'll be five or six years of fighting, and then we'll win, or the Enemy will win, and we'll go along for twenty or thirty years till we have another one. Maybe there won't be any war at all. Perhaps it will be kept in space, and we'll all adjust gracefully to whatever happens out there in the next year or two.

He couldn't feel terrified at the thought of more wars like the ones that had been fought before. It had a reassuring feeling of historical continuity. But he knew it was only his buoyancy of the moment talking. Underneath was the dreadful knowledge that this would be like no war ever fought before—that this would be biblical catastrophe. And with some understanding of how far above the primeval swamps the living organism called civilization towered, how complex and interrelated its physiology, he had an appalling awareness of how far it could fall as it died.

Living things fought with such incredible strength and

tenacity to live—against disease, other living things, the whims of violent nature. And yet, when some invisible level was reached, which passed beyond their limitations, they died with equally incredible ease—including civilizations. Your feelings grow out of watching them deal with things they could more or less cope with.

When something came along just a little stronger, they died with hardly a struggle, and you watched—with uncomprehending horror. He remembered the summer—he was nine—when he discovered that the ant colony under the sidewalk that he had battered ineffectually for four years with water, salt, fire, dirt, rocks, and flyswatters died in satisfying seconds under a half tumbler of kerosene. He remembered his unbelieving confusion. *They must be some other ants. These can't be the ones that were so hard to kill.*

A bomb on one city out of five—probably the country would survive. Two cities out of five...maybe. Three out of five...uh uh. He shuddered.

He forced his mind away from visions of America in her death throes, and discovered he was in the Common. It was quiet here. Three pigeon panhandlers, their heads cocked sagely, looked him over, decided there was no meal here, and moved on to more profitable activities. The hazy blue-green quality of the twilight seemed intensified in the still air among the trees.

In the silence, a woman started to scream—a piercing anguished scream—somewhere nearby. It lasted a few seconds and choked off abruptly, as though a hand had been clapped over her mouth. The sound keened down his spine like an electric shock. He found himself in a half crouch, his ears straining to locate the sound.

It came again, a tiny fragment of a scream, lower in pitch, bubbling with despair, and choked off again.

He had the direction and started to run. As he passed a

cluster of trees, he sighted what he thought were two figures in motion against a low clump of bushes about a hundred yards away. In the uncertain twilight, they looked like two men doing some weird kind of dance.

There was a flash of gold, as a girl's head twisted, and the scene lit up for him as though a spotlight had been turned on... *blonde hair in a pony tail! Ann Fitzgerald!*

There *were* two of them. One held her arms behind her. The other grabbed the hem of her dress with both hands, and in one powerful motion, ripped it completely off, releasing it at the top of his motion to flutter down behind him in a pink and green shimmer, like a dancer's scarf. He bent again to grasp and lift her ankles while the one holding her arms, unkempt dark hair down over his eyes, pulled her head back and lowered her to the grass.

Alan had a torturing glimpse of Ann's white legs stark amidst the greenery.

He was running low and silently, like an animal, completely unaware of the growl deep in his chest. He never knew where he had picked up the rock in his hand. He was about fifteen yards away when the one holding Ann's arms tossed the hair from his face. Their eyes locked for a frenzied instant. The man snarled a warning to his companion as he jumped to his feet.

But the other, engrossed, was still bent over Ann's struggling body. Alan ran up to them. He aimed a kick at the back of the bending man's head as he dove for the one who was standing. He was clawing for the young beast's neck, and would have torn his throat out with his bare hands, if the rock hadn't prevented it.

He felt a numbing blow on the side of his head, and his vision danced. The momentum of his charge had carried him right into the man, and as he threw a punch at the snarling face before him, the man went down, with Alan on top. He felt a pain in his hand, sharp, agonizing. But he still had the rock as he spun, to find the one he had kicked, staggering, stooped over, and dazedly holding his head.

As Alan started for him, he came out of his fog and fled into the gloom. Alan threw the rock after him and felt an excruciating pain dart up his arm.

The young thug he had hit was unconscious, blood covering the side of his face from an ugly cut at the temple. Ann was still lying on the ground, sobbing uncontrollably, her head rolling from side to side, her body very white in the darkness. He bent over her, and untied the rag from her mouth.

"It's all right now, honey," he whispered reassuringly. "It's all right. It's all right. It's me, Alan."

Her eyes unglazed into anger… "The filthy, loathsome—" A shudder traveled her entire body and she settled into a new spasm of sobbing.

Alan helped her to her feet. She covered herself with the remnants of the dress, and he put his jacket over her bare shoulders. He tied the thug's hands with the rag, kicked him to consciousness, and dragged him to his feet. He was only a kid—eighteen or nineteen—and his face was pure hatred. He tried to kick Alan when he turned to Ann, but Alan instantly knocked him down again to a new stab of agony in his hand.

It seemed to take him hours to get the two of them out of the Common, his arm around Ann's waist, the kid just in front, mouthing a steady stream of obscenity and abuse. He turned the kid over to a policeman, along with the story of what had happened, and agreed to come to the station as soon as possible to prefer charges. He flagged a helicab and took Ann home, her teeth chattering now with aftershock.

He left her with a stiff drink, promising to return as soon as he had finished at the police station and walked over to Berkeley Street, thinking over what had happened. There was something tugging at his mind—a feeling of important information buried in the experience. He kept seeing the kid tossing his head up from Ann's struggling body, his eyes turning instantaneously from savage desire to blinding hatred.

The proceedings at the police station took less than half an hour. Alan recounted the incident into a polyrecorder, watching with interest as the graphs faithfully registered the ebb and flow of his emotions through the story. Two officers led the prisoner in and stood him before the lieutenant in charge.

The wound on the youth's temple had been sealed, but the implacable hatred on his face remained as though carved in. While they re-played Alan's statement, he looked slowly and coldly around the room, meeting the eyes of the eight people present with a calm intensity, like a caged panther. Two of the men and the woman looked away under his defiant stare.

When the statement was finished, the lieutenant informed the prisoner of his rights to a psychologist and a lawyer. The kid continued to stare at him, and said nothing. He said nothing when the lieutenant asked him who he was, and where he lived and explained what would follow conviction for attempted rape—six months of psychotherapy at the Cambridge Institution for Rehabilitation, and if judged incorrigible—"resistant"—ten years in the State Institution of Restraint.

Even when a fingerprinting expert arrived to identify him as Francis Garvey of Third Street, South End—and when Records tagged him with seven counts of loitering and disturbing the peace, two of vandalism, two of resisting an officer, two helicar thefts, one count of rape—at age twelve and one of attempted rape, his expression remained unchanged.

The lieutenant, who had been trying in a surprisingly gentle way to reach the youth, gave up as he heard the record.

His shoulders settled slightly. The kid's IQ was 140. He had spent most of his life from fourteen on in Juvenile Institutions of Restraint. Three periods of psychotherapy were all labeled "resistant." He ordered the prisoner taken back to his cell. Garvey shrugged off the hands of the two officers and preceded them out, looking as remote and defiant as when he had come in.

Walking back, Alan kept thinking about Garvey. There was something about his manner that intrigued him—an isolated completeness, more catlike than human. In an almost absolute sense the youth had been formed in the mold of the jungle. Everybody is your enemy. Life is yours on loan, for only as long as you can protect it.

And he'd beaten this jungle animal—and another like him! Alan's shoulders squared unconsciously, as he remembered the brief violence—his own incredible anger. Yes, there had been a tinge of fear way down underneath it, too. His thoughts shifted to Ann. It had been a terrible ordeal for her. She was ordinarily so self-possessed, with a child's faith in the basic goodness of others.

She met him at the door—she had discarded the torn dress and his heart pounded at the sight of her—and clung to him with a mixture of little-girl dependence and clear-eyed longing that matched and reinforced his own feelings like a mirror image. They were in each others arms before he had even closed the door.

CHAPTER TEN

IF IT HADN'T been for the peculiar quality of perceptiveness that alternately irritated and fascinated him in Ann, Alan Kerr might have gone back into the twenty-four-hour turmoil of the labs without ever capturing the vagrant thought that was teasing at the edge of his consciousness.

An hour after his return, they were sitting over bacon and eggs in the kitchenette, talking out the terror of the experience in the park. Alan had done his best to ease the shock within her, but she sensed after a moment that he was preoccupied.

She paused in the middle of pouring him a cup of coffee to look down at him quizzically. "You're somewhere else, aren't you?" she said.

He stared into the half-filled cup and drew a long breath. "I can't get over that kid Garvey. His father was a drunkard—disappeared when the kid was eight or nine years old, and hasn't been heard from since. His mother is in the State Institution For Non Curable Insane—paranoid. The kid has been outside the law ever since he could act for himself. He hasn't a real friend in the world. I doubt if he could even understand what the word means. And yet he's as tough and complete as a wildcat.

"At the station it was like an allegory. There were seven men and a woman in the room. The whole weight of his society was arrayed against him. I found myself starting to feel sorry for him—looking for a flicker of regret, or fear, or even concern that I could sympathize with. But all that showed was this pure flame of hatred and defiance. The police were pretty decent, too. A couple of them were trying hard to reach the kid. It sounds odd, but there was a kind of unity and invulnerability about him that I couldn't help admiring."

He didn't notice Ann's face stiffening as he talked. Three different times she recoiled as though he had slapped her face. Then all at once there was a short, screaming hysterical outburst, and he found himself standing dazed outside the apartment, still hearing her sobs as she slammed the door on him, her accusing words echoing in his head:

"Admiring an animal who hasn't as speck of decency, or respect, or fear of God in him." *Hasn't a speck of decency, or respect, or fear of God, or fear of God, or fear, or fear, or FEAR!*

He was halfway home before he realized why she'd been so furious…why she'd thrown him out.

Alan wrestled with the idea for three days, before he decided to talk it over with the project head. The thing was so outlandish he was afraid he'd be laughed out of the office, or worse, relieved for lab fatigue. But the more he thought about it, the surer he became that he had an answer. Not *the* answer, but a solution good enough to gain them some of the time they needed so desperately.

Dr. Murchison's face was lined and weary with the months of failure. He snapped out a preoccupied, "Good morning, Alan," and looked impatient.

Alan started to change his mind, and then thought of the casualty figures. He took a deep breath. "I have an idea I'd like to try. You'll probably think it's crazy. But if it works, it will give us some time we can use."

He had at least succeeded in gaining Murchison's attention. The chair squeaked loudly as the lab director leaned back. He said benignly, "Nobody's going to think you're crazy, Alan. Most really new ideas sound crazy when we first hear them. And we respect your capabilities perhaps more than you do yourself."

Alan looked down, looked up, and blurted it out. "I'd like

to try resistant juvenile criminals as combat crews."

Murchison's chair came down against his desk with a crash. "Have you gone crazy?" he quietly roared. Then, just as suddenly, he smiled. "Okay, let's hear it."

"Out loud, it's a pretty thin line of reasoning, but it developed out of some ideas I've been kicking around ever since I first got into psychology. It has a validity for me that goes beyond what I can put into words."

Alan described the attack on Ann the previous Sunday, and the way he had been fascinated by Francis Garvey. While he talked, Murchison pulled a gigantic Oom Paul pipe from a drawer in his desk, inspected it fondly, and plunged it into the humidor on his desk, stuffing it to the brim with one hand. He grunted his approval when Alan came to the part about how Ann had ordered him out of the apartment.

Alan went on. "Back in the forties and fifties, there was a husband and wife team named Glouck who did an elaborate study of the patterns of development of first-grade children, correlating behavior characteristics with the types of emotional difficulty that developed later.

"They found that the behavior patterns that indicate future delinquency were completely different from those that foretold neurosis. As you probably know, their work was the basis for the Disturbed Children Program they finally installed last year in the primary schools here in Massachusetts.

"Anyway, reading their work, I couldn't help feeling that the kids tended to fall into one group or the other, according to the amount of inherent physiological and psychological drive they had available, to resist the various pressures they were subjected to. One kid with repressive parents might become vicious and defiant of all authority. Another in the same situation might become—squashed in on himself, meek and neurotic.

"A water buffalo and an ox may be closely related biologically, and may weigh about the same, but their endocrine systems—their entire nervous systems—are inherently different. One is organized for attack, the other for docility." He paused, as Murchison took the pipe out of his mouth. But the director merely inspected it thoughtfully and replaced it between his teeth."

Alan paused, reached for a cigarette, lit it, and went on. "The more I thought about it, the more I became convinced that the kids who became delinquents, outlaws, who fought back against domination—at least the ones who fought back openly—were by heredity a higher drive group than those who surrendered and became civilized. And beyond a certain point, the only way out is surrender. There is no tyranny more complete than that available to a parent.

"Lawlessness, you see, is a man fighting against a tyranny that oppressed him when he was a child—a tyranny that no longer exists. Since it's an irrational fight against a non-present-time threat, it's insatiable. A kid starting out by sassing his teacher can be drawn irresistibly to the point where he kills, and dies snarling at the police, unless at some point he surrenders, and admits to himself that he hasn't the guts to rebel beyond this point.

"I've never had much personal experience with completely hostile kids, though—not until this thing the other evening. It's just been a set of ideas I carried around to play with in the back of my mind when there was nothing better to do. But watching that Garvey kid transmuting everything into anger brought the whole thing back to mind."

Murchison had been listening with an unreadable expression, his arms overlapped behind his neck, puffing infrequently at the huge pipe. He disengaged it now from his teeth, to ask: "How does all this relate to the problem we are attempting to solve?"

Alan continued, surer of himself, laying his sentences down carefully, one by one, like a man building a tower of matchsticks. "The key to the whole problem is fear. Whatever the device they're using, we know the enemy is disorganizing our crews with fear. Pure, basic, across-the-board fear. And if we can stop the fear now, we'll have the time to figure out how they do it later.

"There are only three conceivable kinds of people without fear," he went on slowly. "Some outlaws, some psychotics and, hypothetically, those who have never learned to fear. Psychotics are out, obviously. Men raised so perfectly that they'd never learned to fear? I've never seen one in all the hundreds of men I've Screeped. There's no way of telling if such an individual would have enough drive to resist this radiation, or whatever it is, but I'd be happy to try them if you can find any.

"But here's the point I'm getting at. These defiant kids are so completely conditioned to hostility—so completely adjusted to living in a world of enemies that the fear response is completely short-circuited into anger. Their defiance is proof in itself that they have the drive to resist the things that the rest of us either haven't been exposed to, or that we surrendered to in the process of becoming civilized.

"I realize that there are better ways for a man to face the Enemy than in uncontrollable anger, but it's a giant step forward from fear. And I believe that we can choose crews from among these resistant kids who will transmute whatever it is the Enemy is using, directly into anger, without succumbing to the fear that's cutting our crews down." Alan paused, studying Murchison's face.

The project head had listened with polite interest, giving no sign of his reaction. He turned his heavy bulk now, to stare out of the window, and finally spoke over his shoulder. "You think we're civilized only out of fear?" he asked. "That there is no inherent pleasure in getting along with each other?"

Alan wondered vaguely whether Murchison was simply humoring him or sparring for time to think, but he stuck by his guns. "Of course there's pleasure in getting along with each other—*after* we've learned the rules—*after* we're civilized. But I'm talking about kids who never buckle under—who don't buy the rules in the first place."

Murchison swung to stare full into Alan's eyes. His voice was low, but his words hit with a physical impact, like the blows of a battering ram. "So you want to fight the Enemy with Resistant Juveniles—kids with no fear. Well let me tell you a few things about these kids.

"Let's assume you're right. Some of them have no fear. You know what that means? No organism without a fear mechanism—I don't care whether it's missing genetically, or missing by reason of some sort of psychic amputation due to violent experiences—can be considered sane. These kids are nuts. Psychotic. Out of contact with reality. And you know what that means?"

The bit of Murchison's pipe was jabbing savage furrows in the already tattered desk blotter. "It means the first time they get their hands on a ship, they're just as likely to blow up one of our orbit stations—and a dozen ships and crews with it— as not!"

Murchison realized suddenly he was shouting. He scowled at himself and leaned back in his chair. He continued in a slightly more conversational bellow. "Look: a man without fear is unteachable. He is incapable of conceiving of any consequence of any act of his yielding his own destruction. I don't have to tell you what it takes to be a combat pilot. The coordination, the singleness of purpose. The emotional stability. The devotion to duty…"

His head shook slowly and earnestly. "My God, the

devotion to duty. And the basic intelligence. I don't have to tell you what it takes. How many months have you put in combing the finest kids in the country for these qualities? If they haven't got it, there's no Screep in the world that can give it to them. As desperate as we are for men, you're flunking three out of five. And these kids are *trying*, with everything they've got."

Murchison paused to light his pipe again, using a big, old-fashioned wooden match. "I know the situation is bad, Alan—perhaps I know it better than you do. But unless you can show me a safe—and I mean *safe*—way to teach the things our boys have to know—and be—to kids with no sense of responsibility, no conscience, no fear of punishment, no need to earn the liking and respect of their fellows, I'm afraid we'll have to pass this one up."

It was very silent in the office when the director finished. His last words seemed to reverberate around the room. Alan felt weary and discouraged. This was the problem that had nearly kept him from coming in with the idea at all. Every time he'd thought of what he knew about resistant juveniles, he'd shuddered, convinced he must be getting lab fatigue if he could even dream of such a suggestion.

And yet, when he thought of Garvey, the individual, he felt the same flash of confidence. In a span of a few seconds after Murchison finished, Alan had gone back over a lifetime of work and thought, and have arrived again at the conviction that Garvey would work out.

He held up an index finger. "Not *kids*, Dr. Murchison. *One* kid. One I've had a chance to get a feeling of. For the time being, I'll settle for just this one. He's a holy terror, but there isn't a trace of slyness in him. The chances are very strong that if we asked him, he'd tell us to take our project and go to the devil. But if I can find the buttons to get him to try it at all—reasons that matter to *him*—then he'll go all the way for us. Or at the worst, if he decides he's had a bellyful, he'll tell us so and quit…unless we push him into a corner, of course, and believe me, I have no appetite for pushing him into a corner."

Alan Kerr got up and began to walk the carpet in his characteristic slouch, intent only on getting across the ideas he'd carried bottled up for so long. "Garvey is no more psychotic than I am. He's in magnificent contact with the reality he'd been brought up in. You know as well as I do that the words 'nuts', 'insane', 'psychotic' aren't a neat basket that some of us fall into and some don't. Most psychotics have sane areas…lucid periods. And most of us 'normals' have characteristics that extend toward the psychotic. At this moment there are thousands of people moving into psychosis and thousands of others moving out. You and I have been in this business too long to be frightening ourselves with labels.

"The problem of Juvenile Resistants in general, and Garvey in particular, is a lot more complex than just hanging a label on him. I'm definitely against the pat labeling of a man as psychotic or normal, as though he carried a sandwich board on his back, so that all we have to do is read the label and we have the man pegged like a butterfly on a specimen board.

"And while I'm touching on this I'd like to say something else about the folly that some psychologists engage in when they are discussing a man's emotional adjustment to society in general. It helps to illustrate what I mean, even though it does not directly apply to Garvey himself. It is often taken for granted that your emotionally immature individual is dominated by the so-called pleasure principle and has never learned to subordinate his drive toward immediate pleasurable gratification to some immeasurably larger aim, some ultimate goal or level of achievement that will benefit both himself and society and payoff far more handsomely in the long run.

"But suppose a person reaches so high a level of intellectual discernment that he seriously questions the value of all truly long-range human objectives in a cosmic sense? Suppose he decides that all life on Earth is ultimately meaningless, that we are, as Bertrand Russell one phrased it, 'flyspecks of matter on a midget planet in space?' Suppose he decides, both intellectually and emotionally, that nothing can offer the kind of man he is greater rewards than an immediate surrender to all the delights of the physical world, as the great poets envisioned such delights?

"Suppose he becomes a deliberate, enlightened hedonist— or a cynical hedonist, if you prefer the term—and lets the chips fall where they may, lets the world stew in what he considers to be its own intolerable juices? That may be a philosophy of absolute fatalism, perhaps and I'm not saying I agree with it. But can you honestly label such a man as emotionally immature?"

Alan held up an index finger again and poked it within inches of Murchison's face. "It's important to remember that even so great an idealist as Freud himself—and he was an idealist, a perfectionist in the matter of human behavior— said toward the end of his life that your truly enlightened man may very well decide to live for only two things—women and money. He deplored the fact, but had the intellectual honesty to face up squarely to the possibility.

"So, I feel, it's the height of folly to attempt to pin definite labels on people at all. But to get back to Garvey, take this business of no fear. I can see that's what's bothering you the most, even though it might give us the answer we're looking for. It isn't that the *capacity* to fear is absent—a hereditary abnormality. It's simply that he's been so conditioned by his environment that he passes through the stage where you or I would feel fear…almost instantaneously. Though I *am* convinced that higher hereditary 'drive,' level of energy generation or what have you, correlates with less-fear-response—more anger response.

"To me, fear is awareness of a survival threat plus uncertainty. Uncertainty as to the extent of the threat, or your ability to handle it. The uncertainty is the key. And when a kid grows up in a world in which he knows there is no love, no rewards for good behavior, and no such thing as a friend, then there isn't much uncertainty. He just assumes that everybody is his enemy and proceeds accordingly. The fellow who said: 'I'll take care of my enemies, but Lord, please protect me from my friends,' knew what he was talking about."

A faint smile crossed Murchison's face, and he relaxed a little, swinging again to the window.

Alan continued without even noticing. "This is what I've been describing as a short-circuited fear response. You and I ordinarily assume that other people mean us no harm. When we meet hostility, we rise into anger reluctantly, more or less slowly. We're trying to decide whether it really is hostility, hoping we were mistaken. We're wishing we didn't have to get angry. We're trying to evaluate the extent of the hostility; and trying to judge how much and what kind of a response will be necessary to deal with the threat. This is the matrix in which fear forms. If a fight starts, then most of the uncertainty is removed from the situation, and the fear disappears with it.

"But a Resistant like Garvey has a peculiar advantage here. No uncertainty. He *knows* everybody is his enemy. He has a relay in his head that clicks over whenever he sees a threat—which is practically all the time—and says: 'attack!'. There's no period of uncertainty. But it isn't a hereditary abnormality. It's a conditioned reflex."

Alan scuffed pensively at the rug, and turned to face

Murchison. "I'm aware that the word to describe this kind of a person is 'paranoid', but as long as he's sufficiently in contact with reality to see me as Alan-Kerr-his-enemy, rather than Daddy-his-enemy, or Society-his-enemy, then there is a basis for dealing with him, in terms of his self interest, as he sees it. I'd appreciate the chance to try."

He finished, and stood waiting.

Murchison's head bent to scrutinize his pipe. He examined it carefully on both sides, scraped at a speck with an exploring thumbnail. Finally his eyes lifted under the heavy brows to stare full at Alan, and Alan knew suddenly why he was the project head.

"This Garvey is in an Institution of Restraint now. I suppose you realize how many strings would have to be pulled to make him available, and what might happen if such a project got out of hand. I still say you can't trust one of them with your back turned. It might not turn out well for your career."

"If we don't lick this problem, there may not be any career." Alan sensed a victory he was no longer sure he wanted to win. "I'll forget about locating and training others like him till I see whether he works out. He may not make much of a pilot, but Doctor Murchison, I'll stake my reputation that he won't be dangerous if he's handled right."

The director smiled unpleasantly. "You *are* staking your reputation, Dr. Kerr. And have you thought about how long it might take to train one of these monkeys to operate a space ship?"

"I've been talking to some of the pilot instructors. I have some ideas about teaching him only the combat pass, and using the regular pilots to take him out and bring him back."

Murchison screwed up his face; and sighed heavily, as though he wished he were somewhere else.

"Alan, I don't believe you'd be willing to gamble with a

thing like this if the situation weren't so desperate," he said. "I'm desperate, too. You have a brilliant record, and I feel obligated to go along with you. But remember one thing. This is your project, and your responsibility. If anything goes wrong—you're the goat. Think it over. If you want to go ahead, submit a requisition for what you think you'll need, and I'll see that you get it."

As Alan started to thank him, Murchison cut him off. He said, "Oh…one more thing. You don't Screep him. You're too valuable to lose the way we lost Wagner, with that project of his on manics for isolated duty. Fair enough?"

Alan nodded and when he left his thoughts were far from triumphant.

CHAPTER ELEVEN

THE CLEAN CONCRETE lines of the Massachusetts State Institution of Restraint towered out of the ancient, festering slums of Charlestown like a magnificent oak in a town dump. Sharp-edged vertical stripes of greenish shadow and bright orange in the crisp October morning gave no hint of the building's grim purpose—the restraint of sane men who could not be allowed to live at large, yet who could not be rehabilitated by any currently available method. Put simply…restraint. A society's visible admission of failure.

And yet, Alan Kerr mused, looking down at the functional mass of the building, it was actually progress. He could still remember the uproar on the teletypes when Governor Kennedy had first demanded that state institutions of incarceration be separated according to their true functions— for the curable, and the incurable; for rehabilitation, for restraint, and for punishment, too, if the legislators wanted it that way. It was amazing how much progress and enlightenment had come out of such a seemingly simple change.

The idea of a penal system, for punishment, had vanished in the self-searching discussions that had followed, of what to do with those who were judged unfit to live among their fellow men.

The soft hum of the helicab dropped to a lower note as the cabbie started down, and Alan's thoughts returned to the purpose of his trip. He was nervous about seeing Garvey, and he made no bones about admitting it to himself. It was absolutely vital that the youth go along with the project Alan had so laboriously organized in the past week. On sober reflection, he had been forced to the conclusion that screening unwilling resistants to locate those with an adequate hate reflex was not only impossible in the time at his disposal, but would stir up a political hornet's nest he couldn't handle.

And since he would be dealing with resistants, Screep evaluations would be undependable, anyway. The only way to tell how they would behave under stress would be to study them under stress, which would be awkward, to say the least. The only one he was sure of was Garvey. It had to be Garvey. But the odds were he'd simply tell Alan to take his project, and blow it out his briefcase.

He went over, once more, the strategy, he'd decided on as the only approach that had a chance of success, checking each point in order. It would have to be a straight, blunt offer of a trade. Any sign of softness, or attempted friendship, would convince Garvey that he was being suckered. And the first misstep would be the last.

The cabbie dropped the last twelve feet. He caught the cab a few inches above the roof, turning Alan's stomach upside down in the process and set down as lightly as a feather. When he turned around expecting admiration, Alan rewarded him with a scowl that instantly withered the grin on his face.

Two guards inspected Alan's collection of passes—seven in all—while two other guards with drawn guns watched alertly. From the way they traded glances, they knew something about his visit, but they offered no comment and asked for none. One, who seemed from his manner to be the ranking guard, said: "Follow me, Dr. Kerr." And started for the elevator head, while the others, still almost ludicrously vigilant, watched the cab safely off.

The guard led Alan directly from the elevator to a large but plainly furnished office with the single word, SUPERINTENDENT, on the door. The warden, George Scanlon, making no pretense of being occupied, was seated at a desk absolutely clean except for a single folder and a small PV intercom. He rose as they entered, looking Alan over shrewdly as he dismissed the guard. His manner was courteous, but Alan had the feeling the man was somewhat surprised to find such an unprepossessing intellectual at the end of the chain of influence that had been applied during the past four days.

Alan took a seat in the chair he offered, and discovered he was facing an entire wall of PV screens, four banks high and ten rows wide, most of them in operation, showing various scenes throughout the institution.

The interview lasted about five minutes, with Scanlon doing most of the talking. He was attempting, not too subtly, to learn what they were planning to do with Garvey. Alan murmured a few generalities about tests of new psychological equipment, and Scanlon, visibly put off, launched into a discussion of what these restrainees were like, and how they should be handled. Alan remembered little of it, most of his attention leaping on ahead toward the approaching session with Garvey. Amidst the panorama of PV screens surrounding him he found himself wishing the warden would finish so that he could get on with his mission.

And finally, the moment was at hand, with Scanlon himself escorting Alan by elevator and staircase, through at least a dozen barred doorways into a separate gallery, surrounded by tiers of barred cells. Looking upward, Alan could see that each tier overhung the one below it, and the walkway in front of each tier was mounted on massive hinges, so that it could be lowered hydraulically, leaving any given cell or group of cells in complete isolation.

Garvey's cell was in the next to the top tier. Scanlon introduced Alan with: "This gentleman is here to see you. If there's any trouble, you'll pay for it." He turned to Alan and said, "When you're ready to leave, call the guard."

The cell was more comfortably furnished than Alan had expected it would be. There was an easy chair, bolted to the floor, with a lamp for reading mounted in the wall behind a grille. Beside a tiny stone sink, also set into the wall, was an open steel structure of four shelves, forming a sort of open bureau, with a sheet of polished steel bolted to the wall at the top, serving as a mirror. There were two books on the top shelf of the bureau.

Garvey was lying on the cot. They recognized each other in an instantaneous locking of eyes that tingled the back of Alan's neck in recollection.

They studied each other speculatively while the guard's footsteps died away. Finally, Alan said: "Hello Garvey."

The other nodded almost imperceptibly, not taking his eyes off Alan's face.

"I've got a deal for you that could get you out of here. Are you interested?"

An equally imperceptible shrug.

"I'm with the Human Resources and Training Division, Garvey." Alan had a submerged awareness that calling him Francis would arouse his hostility. "We'd like to try you out as a space ship pilot. How does that sound?"

Garvey looked away, to stare at the ceiling. "Sounds like a snow job."

Score one. I've got a response out of him. Alan's eyes brightened. "Let's put it this way. If it weren't...a snow job, would you be interested?"

"Keep talkin'."

"Okay, Garvey, here it is. We're having some trouble with our crews. The Enemy has been doing something that makes them scared in combat. I don't care much for you, but I have an idea you don't scare easily. So I'm trying to get permission to test you in the job. If you work out, we'll try others like you. I thought you might like the first crack at it."

For the first time, Garvey showed emotion, coming up on one elbow. "What kind of a moron do you think I am—to buy that kind of baloney?"

Alan's face hardened. "Okay, Garvey, if that's the way you want it." He walked to the bars to call the guard.

"Wait a minute, Doc. While you're here, let's hear the rest of the pitch."

Score two. He took the hook. Alan congratulated himself on his planning. He sauntered over to the bureau and thumbed through the two books. Hobbs' *Spacecraft of All Nations*, and a catalog of weird and ostentatious designs and accessories for helijets.

What a break. He's a hot-rodder!

He turned and sliced the air savagely. "There isn't any pitch, Garvey. I'm not foolish enough to think you give a damn that your country needs you—though it does. But it's a chance to get rid of your past—to wipe the slate clean, and get a fresh start, if that means *anything* to you... You'll have the right to kill—legally."

Their eyes were locked again, Alan's flashing, Garvey's cold and hooded. "You haven't killed yet, have you Garvey? But at the rate you're going, you will before too long. And they'll catch you, and lobotomize you, and put you away for the rest of your natural life. Do you know what lobotomy is?"

He grunted as Garvey's eyelids flickered in recognition. "Maybe when you've killed a few of the Enemy you'll have enough of the poison out of your system to settle down and live like a human being among the rest of us."

He threw his ace. "If you're good enough, that is. There are a lot of good men getting killed out there. Better men than you, with years of training. You'll have to do it in months—almost weeks. And if you get killed, nobody will know about it, or care.

"But it's an honest to God chance to be a hero, complete with all the fixings—medals, banquets, beautiful girls and all." Venomously he added, "You won't have to jump them in the Common, either. They'll be chasing you."

Garvey slid his legs off the cot, and sat up slowly. He rested his elbows on his knees and stared at the floor for several minutes. Finally he said in an almost inaudible voice, "I'll think it over."

Alan hid his exultation. "I'm sorry Garvey. We've got just three months to find out if you have what it takes. There simply isn't time for thinking it over. If it can't be you, it will have to be someone else. I tried you first because I know you."

Both faces lightened in unison, not nearly a smile, but a definite sharing of humor that softened the hard tension in the cell. "And I know you're hard enough to be the man I'm looking for. I couldn't come back and ask you again, even if I wanted to. Will you do it?"

Garvey's stare traveled slowly down Alan's body, rested on his feet for a long moment, and traveled slowly up again. He said, "If you're suckerin' me, Doc, I promise I'll kill you."

Alan checked an impulse to offer his hand—covered it up by going to the bars and calling the guard. He turned. "It's a deal Garvey. You'll be leaving here tomorrow. Get ready for the hardest work you've ever done in your life."

They waited for the guard in silence, each staring off into his own thoughts, ignoring the other.

CHAPTER TWELVE

THE SCREEP SANG its inaudible music; Garvey mumbled his unending river of vicious obscenity; and the walls of the room were wavering and growing dim again. Alan wondered desperately for the hundredth time, why he had let himself in for this agony. Doggedly he turned the gain up a notch, threw out a tendril of fear, and repeated: "Your father, your father, your father..."

Back came the terrible pounding smashing hammer of hate, no matter how he set himself he was never ready for it, hate and filth and turmoil pouring and flooding through him and pushing down with incredible irresistible power—down into his bowels until every cell cringed and crawled, numbing him and draining the strength out of him, strangling him, he was lost, lost in an ocean of hate, the whole universe hating him, was there no end to it, there had to be an end, there had to be an end!

And suddenly, it had ended. There was a blessed quiet and the air was sweet in his nostrils. Every bone and muscle writhed in sheer relief. He heard someone say: "I think he's coming out of it," and opened his eyes.

For an instant, the three figures around him seemed to tower foggily, forty feet above his crib. Then the room snapped back into focus, and he discovered he was lying on the Screep Room cot, looking up at Dr. Murchison and two lab technicians. Garvey sat slouched, still in the loveseat, gazing at him under lowered brows with a look of respect, almost of compassion.

Alan blinked and sat up painfully. Every inch of his body tingled and stung as though it had been pounded by mallets. He became aware that nobody in the room was saying anything because of Garvey's presence, and was grateful. His voice was thin and strange when he spoke. "Okay, Garvey, I guess that's it for today. It's about time for your simulated pilotage, anyway."

Murchison waited impatiently until the door closed behind Garvey. "Damn it Alan," he said. "You've been working with him for three weeks, and this is the fourth time he's blanked you out. You started this thing against my better judgement in the first place. I have to admire your guts, but do you mind if I ask what's the point? You know Resistants don't Screep. By your own theory, half of what makes this kid a good bet is his hate reflex, and you're killing yourself trying to knock it out of him. There'll be no more of this, understand? *He* is just another Resistant kid, but I can't replace *you*."

Alan smiled ruefully. "I know. You're right. I'm not even sure what I've been trying to do. It's just that he's probably going to go out and get killed, and we had to sit around and wait anyway, while he learned pilotage, and I was hoping to learn something about the hate reflex that we could use. But he's too much for me. We'll just have to let him go, and try to learn from the way he performs. How's he coming as a pilot?"

"I was just talking with Jenkins. He's been working him six hours a day in the space trainer. He says Garvey's a natural. Completely free of the bashfulness toward the equipment that slows most of them down. He's taking him out for actual space work next week. He figures that with two or three weeks of practice out at station, on a real ship, the kid should be able to run a combat pass well enough to get by. He's arranged for Paul Coulter—he's an old pro, one of the best they've got—to serve as navigator-pilot. He'll take the ship out, and berth it, and generally run things. In between...well, the kid will have plenty of chance to prove himself."

Murchison paused, and his lips tightened. "I might add that Coulter is a volunteer, and none of us will feel too good if this thing doesn't work out. If you've seen anything, working with Garvey, to change your mind about him, nobody would have anything but respect for you if we dropped it now."

Alan ran a hand through his hair and squeezed the back of his neck. "The only thing I've changed my mind about was my hope that I could work him with the Screep. He's full of junk, but he's smart, and he simply doesn't know how to be afraid. I'm still betting on him."

It was hard to tell whether Murchison was relieved or disappointed. He shrugged; indicated with a quick nod of his head that it was still Alan's responsibility; and departed.

Francis Garvey stood tall in the cradle—flexed his shoulder muscles, stretching against the harness—and inhaled deeply, enjoying the luxurious feeling that he owned everything he saw. His eyes wandered over the cockpit—the controls that responded to his hand, the instruments and gauges that spoke to him—and he understood. The sightscreen, waiting patiently in the center of the panel before him. Behind him was the whole sleek and shining and deadly ship. *His* ship.

His gaze swung out through the row of ports, noting how the shadow curving across the nose of the ship disclosed slight unevennesses in the metal skin. He smiled at the way the impenetrable shadow curtained off part of Betsy's body— a brazen, legged nude, painted in brash lines and colors by some lonesome technician in his off hours—making her look suddenly bashful, as though she were hiding coyly behind a shower drape.

He looked out to the vault of the heavens, drinking in the blazing millions of stars, still vaguely surprised that the sky was black. After four weeks of training and two combat patrols, he still felt slightly shocked that it wasn't the shining blue of a sunny day on earth—shocked, but excited in a way that the brightest blue couldn't have excited him. Far over at the edge of a port was a thin sliver of moon, close enough so he could see the jagged edge of the umbra. The moon was his, too.

Boy, this was the life, floating along, taking things easy, enjoying the view, far away from those insignificant bastards on Earth—he was aware of the planet rolling along beneath his feet, though he couldn't see it. From a childhood game, a phrase came back to roll around in his mind...*King of the world...King of the world.*

Absorbed in his own well being, he started at the sudden hiss of power, then grinned as Coulter's voice in the intercom informed him he was about to see some action. "No practice passes this time, Garvey. I've got a live one. You ready to go to work?"

The nose of the ship dropped viciously, swinging to the right.

"Yeah," he said. "I'm ready."

Garvey's awareness of Coulter's low opinion of him had no effect on his rising excitement. Coulter had made no bones about his conviction that this was the most hare-brained project that had ever left earth.

But he was a good soldier. He'd taught Francis everything he could in the few weeks they'd worked together, warning him several times a day— "The first time you get out of line, I'll take the controls away so fast your head will spin."

As it happened, Garvey's suspicions were correct—that Coulter's orders were not to touch the controls during a pass, except for the direst emergency—but he didn't care much, either way.

"Make your cockpit check; lower air pressure to seven pounds; open the bomb port, and arm your bomb."

Garvey obeyed, swore savagely when his increasing difficulty in breathing reminded him that he hadn't closed his helmet, and slammed the fishbowl down over his head. The sightscreen stayed blank through several minutes of acceleration and coasting, punctuated by Coulter's brutally sudden turns, and then suddenly there was a faint pip at the edge of the screen.

Garvey watched fascinated, as it drifted in toward the bullseye. There was no instructor sitting just outside, feeding that pip into the screen. This was a real one, a ship with men in it whose mission was to kill him. He peered at the inscrutable skies ahead, and back at the screen, feeling the hatred that waited out there. The pip seemed to pulse with a malignance all its own.

Just before the pip reached center, Garvey's head snapped around to the right, utterly without volition. He found himself ready to leap, his hands poised over the harness buckle staring in a raging anger at the spare oxygen bottles hung on the rear wall of the cockpit.

He could have sworn someone or something was watching him, watching with an implacable hatred. As he glared in confusion at the innocent row of bottles, he realized Coulter was speaking. "Do you think that joker is going to wait all day for you to decide whether you want to fly this thing? For Pete's sake, let's go!"

He shook his head to clear it, deciding instantly not to tell Coulter of the weird incident. Coulter was worried enough about him already. He settled himself at the controls and squeezed the throttle mike button.

"Sorry, Cap. I've got her now. How far away are we?"

Coulter was still irritated, but he sounded unsure of himself relieved that Garvey was taking over. "We're about a thousand miles out. I have their velocity neutralized. It'll be about one hundred sixty seconds, if nothing goes wrong. Go in at maximum acceleration. Let your bomb go at a hundred miles—no closer—and get out at maximum acceleration. Understand?"

"In max; let go at a hundred; out max. Nothing to it, Cap. Here we go." He pushed the throttle steadily, all the way to the stop, thrilling to the surge of power as his body squashed heavier and heavier back into the cradle.

The accelerometer read 12 G's. *Around 400 feet per second per second.* For a few seconds he called the velocities off to himself...*1200 feet per second...1600...2000...2400...2800 feet per second...faster than a high powered rifle bullet and only getting started...*and the thing was watching him again—closer! He turned his head to look and the acceleration slammed his face sideways into the cradle. There was nothing there but the oxygen bottles.

With a terrible, superhuman effort he wrenched his head back around again and stood panting in the cradle, staring but not seeing as the gauges tracked the pass. Relative velocity to target, four miles per second—the needle was climbing visibly. Target range about nine hundred miles, in the stretch just under half of full velocity, where the needle then seemed to quiver and crouch for its final leap down the dial.

CHAPTER THIRTEEN

FOR A LONG moment, Francis Garvey was on the verge of what would have been the first and last panic of his life. The evil in the corner watched him, creeping closer, choosing its moment to kill him, while the acceleration pinned him helpless in the cradle. Spiders crawled over his skin, as he fought the impulse to turn and look again.

For a space of perhaps five seconds, he struggled wildly and senselessly to push his ton of weight out of the cradle. He finished spent and gasping, filled with a wild helpless rage, as though he were held by a straitjacket.

Straitjacket. The idea took him back to the first time he'd been caught, when two giant policemen walked him back to the station, holding his arms behind him, and almost carrying him, so that his kicking feet hardly touched the ground.

Like a string of firecrackers, his mind ran up the chain of times he'd been held, through his mother and his father, and the kid gangs, and the innumerable policemen, and the institutions of restraint, to Wills and Tabor, the recruiting truck and the girl on the Common, to Charlestown and Dr. Kerr. He was on familiar ground now, and a molten hatred rose in him that had only one goal—to live long enough to kill Alan.

He settled his hands to the controls, and scanned the instruments quickly. The pip had drifted six degrees off center, and he eased the wheel over to correct it. Long seconds went by and the pip stayed where it was. He swung the wheel over farther, still with no results. He muttered to himself, "The damn screen's stuck."

He spun the wheel viciously, realizing at the same instant that the Enemy was taking evasive action. Outraged, he hollered over the intercom, "Hey, Cap. They're trying to get away from us!"

There was no answer. Coulter sat in his cubicle, huddled in catatonic terror, completely lost somewhere inside himself, bereft of his last anchor to reality—the duty of a pass to be completed.

Garvey's abrupt yank at the wheel had re-established the pursuit curve at the last possible moment. Slowly the pip crawled back to center, and he eased the turn, watching intently, to catch the first sign of movement in the screen. It came again, on the other side of the bullseye, and he corrected again.

The ship drove on—relative velocity to target climbing past 8 miles per second, its increase hardly slowed by the enemy's flight to the side. The lazy shift of the stars was belied by the raw hiss of power and the agonizing acceleration pressure. And Francis Garvey, alone as he had never been alone before (he knew now there would be no help from Coulter) fought to keep a speck of light at the center of a piece of green glass; fought, with wave after wave of hatred, to push back the gathering darkness, to kill the Enemy ship writhing invisibly a few hundred miles in front of him; fought to stay alive long enough to get his hands around Alan Kerr's throat.

The presence behind him was no more than a minor mosquito bite, lost in the torrents of hatred that consumed him—all but a tiny clear intelligence that seemed to direct from over his head, as his eyes read the screen and his hands obeyed.

The scream of the gyros, as he tracked the casts of the Enemy, was the only thing that told him whether he was turning or travelling a straight line. He lived only to extinguish the captive dot of light that tried so hard to escape from the sightscreen. It was getting harder and harder to hold his target, as the streaking ship narrowed the gap. Dimly he recalled Jenkins drawling, "Keep it under five degrees and the bomb'll do the rest." He couldn't hold it under five degrees much longer.

An amber light flickered on in the panel, then steadied, to mark the 200-mile range. About ten seconds to go. He threw the wheel hard over, to stop one last cast of the enemy, couldn't bring the pip back, hung on grimly, to hold it at three degrees, and as the red light flashed on, squeezed the button on the wheel, cursing the bomb out of the ship on a triumphant welling gout of hate.

Ten seconds to get out of the way. It took two of those seconds to get the ship turned sideways. And at a crawling 12 G's, the ship began to inch away from its track.

Behind them, the bomb, a miniature of its mother, traveled in their former course, accelerating at 15 G's. In its nose, the colony of electronic ganglia hummed busily as they tracked the lump of matter ahead, relays clicking cheerfully as they corrected for its sideward movement.

Down in the rocket's belly, the bomb was warm with anticipation. The proximity fuse scanned the skies ahead hungrily, set to go off at the closest point to any object once it got within 400 yards. A clock ticked off the two minutes it would allow the other devices to do their work. And drifting sideways at ten miles per second, SF 582 hurtled along behind its own bomb, two men inside hovering on the edge of unconsciousness, struggling to escape its rendezvous.

Through the haze that ran rampant in his mind, Garvey knew that for better or worse, his job was done. If the Enemy hadn't turned in the same direction at the same moment, they were safe. It was standard tactics, if a ship knew in time that it had been zeroed, to match the attacker's break, in the hope of keeping the detonation close enough to his track to include both ships in the explosion.

The Enemy tried it, but he had hardly gotten turned around before the bomb took him.

Snarling his rage, Garvey searched the sky, hungering for the explosion. He turned his head slightly to the right, and discovered the incredible blinding malignance reaching out for him, expanding like a nightmare, jagged as an octopus in the unconfining void. His sideward velocity was unbelievable. He brought his hands up to cover his face, then stared, hypnotized as the fingers of flame reached for him.

For an instant, it seemed he was falling straight into the mass of fire. Then the ship's forward motion became apparent, and the ugly wound in the sky, corruscating down the spectrum, drifted majestically backwards and across their tail.

In the navigator's compartment, Coulter's eyes returned to awareness. He began to cry, softly at first, and then terrible wracking sobs, like a child.

Garvey killed the throttle and went limp in the cradle, drawing long shuddering breaths. He was exhausted, but underneath the fatigue there was a strange quietness inside him, as though thousands of voices which had been murmuring all his life, busily but unnoticed, had been stilled. The quietness worried him. Perhaps he had burned something out. He explored the feeling cautiously; decided he was as sharp as ever; and realized he was enjoying the quietness very much. *Like having myself to myself for the first time.*

He sighed contentedly, and called Coulter, "How 'bout that! Not bad for a rookie. Huh, Cap?"

There was a long pause before Coulter answered. The intercom failed to disguise the hoarse croak that was his voice, "Not bad, Garvey. Get her headed for home, and I'll take her in."

The relative velocity to station was just about 16 miles-per-second away. Francis rolled the ship over a couple of times before he found the Earth, shining big and warm and friendly in the emptiness of the void. He set course for home at 4 G's, smiling at the strange arithmetic of outer space, which would see them speeding backwards for nearly a quarter of an hour while the rockets were pushing them forward.

He turned, with anticipation born of long experience, to savoring his revenge on Dr. Kerr, and discovered after a few moments, that the subject was tasteless to him. Like a car stuck in a snowdrift, he backed up; took a fresh start; and charged in again, picturing the various pleasant alternatives open to him, for killing Alan. And again, the subject held no pleasure.

Something *had* happened to him! Incredulous, he began to explore deep in his own mind. He tried a few simple multiplications but found all in order, then he and went on to probe his memories, calling up his favorite feuds, the various humiliations he had kept alive for years, carefully nursing the flame of vengeance, all the murders he had dreamed of, the people he had hated the most, back to the landlord who had evicted them and made his mother cry, when he was four.

The memories were all there, but the feelings of hate were gone, washed clean, completely vanished. He felt lonesome without it, and muttered a vicious obscenity to himself, just to show he was as good as ever. He said it again and again. And suddenly something about the picture of himself trying to bring hatreds back to life struck him funny. He chuckled, started to laugh, and was presently pounding the panel with glee, the tears coursing down his cheeks, not knowing whether he was laughing or crying, but enjoying himself hugely.

A little while later, when Coulter wearily docked the ship at station, and killed the fires, Garvey was sound alseep, a blissful, innocent smile on his face.

CHAPTER FOURTEEN

THE FOLLOWING DAY, Garvey asked the station commander for permission to return to Earth. He obviously had something on his mind, but refused to discuss his reasons further than to say he wanted to talk to Dr. Kerr. He had taken enough radiation so that he wouldn't be allowed on a mission for several weeks, but space regulations forbade all but the most urgent transport from station to Earth. His request was radioed to Earth. Bureaucratic wheels spun dizzily, and three hours later Francis was on his way.

The news that Garvey was coming down left Alan with mixed feelings. It had come in at 5 o'clock Saturday afternoon. He had been feeling more and more depressed, and had caught himself several times, lately, wishing he'd compelled Ann to marry him a month before.

He'd been intending to call her, knowing she'd expect to see him that evening, but he was burning with curiosity to learn how the mission had gone. He decided to wait at the lab. He called the spaceport to have Garvey notified where he was; grabbed a quick bite at the cafeteria; and went to work on some overdue reports.

It was nearly midnight before Garvey arrived. Alan had finished his paper work over an hour before, and had been walking the floor of the lab, stopping occasionally to toy with a piece of equipment, or to stare out the windows at the lights of the city across the river, very conscious of the unaccustomed silence in the building.

He heard the elevator doors open and close, and stood waiting by his desk, as the rapid clicking of heels came down the long hall. Garvey didn't bother to knock. He came through the doorway purposefully, then stopped as he saw

Alan.

His face was unreadable, showing a mixture of unfamiliar expressions. He carried himself less guardedly—less as if he expected attack at any second—than Alan remembered. He looked better fed, almost handsome in his ensign's uniform.

Garvey spoke first, his voice lower than Alan remembered it. "Hello, Doc. I came around to say thanks." He smiled a lopsided smile and offered his hand. "About this time yesterday, I was figuring out how to kill you."

"It was that bad, huh?" Alan smiled in return, and suddenly found himself liking this kid. "Feel like telling me about it?"

Francis Garvey tossed his cap on the desk. He scowled thoughtfully. "That's what I wanted to talk to you about. There was something that happened on the pass—something screwy—that I've got some ideas about."

They sat down, and he described the mission, going into careful detail about his feeling that something had been watching from behind him. Alan listened, fascinated, jotting down an occasional note.

Garvey lit a cigarette, and continued. "After I got back, I kept thinking about how the thing seemed to be behind me, but the Enemy was in front of me, and it didn't make sense. Thinking it over, there was something familiar about the way it felt, but I couldn't place it. Then, in the middle of lunch, it came to me that it felt like when we were working with the Screep, only flat—like a machine." He groped for the description. "It didn't have any personality."

Alan nodded. "That sounds like what we've been figuring. They've got some gadget just playing one tune at you, over and over again."

"Yes, but why did it seem to come from behind me?"

Alan opened his mouth and began: "Oh, you probably—" And then, as the idea hit him, he jumped to his feet. "You mean maybe it's still ultrasonics! You say there was nothing on that wall but oxygen bottles?"

"That's right, Doc."

Alan shrugged into his jacket. "Let's go, laddie. You and I are going to find out what's behind those bottles."

An hour and a half later, a disgruntled lieutenant J.G., still irritated at being pulled from a sound sleep, opened the door to a classroom and gestured them inside. He explained for the fourth time that the patrol ship used here for instruction was similar in every important detail to those being used in combat.

There was one helpful difference. The panels were held by thumb-catches, which took only a moment to loosen. The lieutenant watched in growing alarm, as Alan and Garvey pulled out the entire bulkhead at the rear of the cockpit, and stacked the sections in a sprawling pile on the floor. They found themselves staring at a solid wall of electronic equipment, except for a small crawl hole at the lower right.

Alan looked at Garvey. "Where would you say it was?"

Francis Garvey walked over, stood in the cradle, and snuggled himself in. He turned, stared, and pointed. "Right about there," he said.

Alan turned to the lieutenant. "Would you know what that box is?"

"All I can say is it's part of the radar equipment." The officer bent to scrutinize the cabinet, and added in a voice that was a sepulchral echo of his classroom delivery, "This section here"—he outlined about a third of the equipment with his hand—"is the radar. It includes six separate sets, which cover every possible direction of approach, the IFF, and the sightscreen radar and computer."

Alan looked at his watch. It was nearly four o'clock, and he was suddenly aware of how tired he was. He drew a small circle on one of the radar cabinets at the point Garvey had indicated, and asked the lieutenant to get him a map of the equipment, with each section labeled, and the small circle located on it. The lieutenant promised gratefully to send it over the first thing in the morning, and they left him staring unhappily at the wreckage on the floor.

The next week was a nightmare. Alan had a long conference with Murchison on Sunday morning, outlining the possibilities Garvey's report had opened up, and organizing the new attack on the problem. They called the Navy, to pass on the hopeful news, and to recommend that the suspected equipment be examined immediately on every ship in the fleet, to guard against the off chance of sabotage.

And then they spent two days in a running PV conference with the Navy Base and Washington, on whether the work should be done at the spaceport, or the lab. Murchison finally won out, but only after it was made clear that the Navy would receive generous credit in all news releases.

The news of a possible break had leaked all over the labs. By the middle of Thursday afternoon, when the parts began arriving, everybody in the building was down in the corridor, watching and gossiping, and clogging the hallway. Dr. Murchison tried several times to shoo them back to their own work, but finally gave up as they kept drifting back.

It took the rest of the week to get the ship assembled in the auditorium—the only room in the building large enough to hold it—and the Screep moved in. The ship was set up horizontally, so the 'pilot' could stand in the cradle, as in flight. It squatted in an area where the seats had been cleared out, meek and ungainly looking, yet with an aura of secret deadliness about it.

And on Sunday, they settled to work, a small army of thirteen men (three psychologists, four Screep technicians, and six navy specialists) compared to the three or four Alan was accustomed to. He wasn't happy about it. It gave him an uneasy feeling of things being done that he didn't know about, with so many men running around. But there was no way to avoid it. The job required the pooling of many skills.

Surprisingly enough—to Alan—it was one of the Navy men who cracked the nut, with a small radar transmitter he had rigged, following some ideas of his own. It happened on a Wednesday morning, about a week and a half after they started. Both Alan and Garvey exclaimed "Hey" at the same instant, as a tiny snake's tongue of fear flickered in their brains and was gone.

The whole group froze, as Alan's voice cracked out, "Nobody move! Remember exactly what you're doing!"

And three hours later, after a careful, step by step check of the four men whose work might have been responsible, the entire building was startled, doors opening and heads popping out, as Alan went loping down the corridor hollering at the top of his lungs, "It's the IFF, the IFF, the IFF!"

He burst into Murchison's office and skidded to a stop, as the director looked up, startled, from a handful of papers. He stood near the door, grinning like a college boy on his first binge, and repeated, "It's the IFF."—as though he was explaining why a light bulb had gone out.

Murchison waited for him to go on; put the papers down, to adjust his glasses; and finally said, *"What's* the IFF?"

"Identification of Friend or Foe," said Alan. And then, realizing what Murchison had meant, he poured the story out in one long torrent, with hardly a pause for breath, laughing and bubbling and triumphant with vindicated faith, and the release of months-long anxiety; how the IFF was designed to amplify and to recognize the pattern impressed on a ship's own faint returning radar signal by another ship; how the Enemy, by oscillating their transmittal signal—many times as powerful as the returning allied echo—across the range of the IFF receiver, had built up a vibration in the set, which encompassed bits of the tubes, segments of the chassis, and finally parts of the ship itself, as sounding boards for the ultrasonic pattern of fear; and how the IFF was integral with the radar circuits, to prevent some forgetful navigator from fingering an Allied ship for attack, but all they had to do was to provide an on-off switch for the IFF.

Then Alan was gone, running down the hall again, while Murchison, having uttered not a word, was still reaching for the PV switch.

There was just a little more to it than that. There was an added human factor. It had long been known that the ordinary convolutions of a ship in space disrupt the vestibular apparatus of the human ear to a fairly harmless but far from negligible extent. When equilibrium can be disrupted by any means on a slightly more pronounced scale—a scale that still does not result in actual dizziness or staggering—psychologists have demonstrated that a pattern of well-defined fear in accord with Sorokin's ultrasonics can be generated in a crescendo that mounts and mounts—a fear as absolute and as emotionally crippling as a heavy sword hanging suspended above a man's head.

CHAPTER FIFTEEN

RESEARCH teams, like baseball teams, or other groups of humans sharing a common effort, tend to evolve a folklore, a sort of loose-leaf biography capturing their great moments of triumph, or courage, or humor. For years afterward, legends would still be accumulating around the monumental celebration triggered by Dr. Alan Kerr's dash.

It started with personnel from all over the building drifting into the auditorium to see for themselves the diseased radar and to swap congratulations, titillating themselves again and again with thrills of terror, as they demonstrated the discovery to each new arrival.

Pretty soon, somebody broke out a case of beer, scarce and costly under the second prohibition—the creeping prohibition of local option. Shortly thereafter, closets, cabinets, and desk drawers had disgorged enough alcohol to fuel the party into and through the night. The simplest remarks became uproariously funny. Feuds that had lasted for months washed away in the flood of good will, and lifetime friendships flowered between people who had merely nodded to each other in the corridors.

The barriers of restraint went down between men and women who had worked side by side, wanting each other, week after week. Elevator operators and bearded professors sang bawdy songs, arms about each other's shoulders. It was one of those rare unloadings of tension that seem to occur spontaneously—uncapturable within the confines of plans and arrangements—releasing an immense backlog of irritations and depressions, and leaving the participants, when they recover awareness, feeling newborn, with a euphoria that carries on for weeks.

Sometime during the early evening, Alan and Garvey found themselves telling jokes in a darkened corner of the auditorium, as the party eddied away from them. Alan had been drinking a little and was in that state of anaesthetized inhibition where social intercourse was sheer effortless pleasure, everybody was wonderful, and the divine pattern in the world was clearly visible, in all its shining simplicity.

He clapped Garvey on the shoulder. "You're not a bad kid," he said. "I'm getting to like you. You know, there was a stretch there where I was kind of scared about you. Damn scared. You had a lot of badly crossed-up wiring in you—if you'll forgive the expression. Couldn't tell whether you were going to finish up a hero, or...a bum, and make me one, too. You worked out all right though."

He patted him on the shoulder again. "You worked out splendidly."

Garvey punched him lightly in the biceps. "It wouldn't have happened without you, Doc. I meant it when I said thanks, the other day. You were right about getting out the poison. But if anybody had told me it would all happen in five minutes, even with that gadget pushing me," he flipped a thumb toward the Screep, "I'd have told him he was nuts."

Alan banged him on the shoulder again. His voice had picked up a rolling, oratorical thickness. "That's right, and what you showed us in those five minutes is a damn sight more important than this damn IFF, and their damn war."

His face fell into sorrowful lines, almost humorous in its utter sadness. "Damn Enemy. Serve 'em right if we dropped IFFs all over the place, and blew all the malice out of them in one easy lesson. Then we could get this damn Screep training off our backs, and get back to something worthwhile." Suddenly he smiled. "Hey, that's not a bad idea!" He fumbled for a note pad and scribbled in it, repeating the words as he wrote. "Drop IFF's on the Enemy...what was I talking about?"

Garvey's face screwed up in recollection. "Something worthwhile."

"Something worthwhile!" Alan grasped his lapels with both hands. "Do you realize that with what we learned from you, we can cure Resistants—the real bad ones—do you know what that means? Do you understand the importance? And you gave us the answer.

"Of course," he went on, "you won't be any angel for a long time yet. A man is his data, and if you were brought up in a jungle, then the world is a jungle, not just where you feel, but where you think, too. All your data still says the world is out to get you, even if the anger is gone. It'll be a long time before you can trust people very much."

He followed Garvey's stare across the room to the cute redhead who worked downstairs as a clerk, and chuckled. "That's an interesting piece of new data. You've had your eye on Marilyn all day. Planning on taking her seriously?"

Garvey turned to him with an odd, worried expression. "You think she'd like me?"

"You're kidding...she's nuts about you. You're a hero."

"What should I say? How do I start talking to her?"

"Same as always. Just say what comes into your mind."

"But how do I...?"

Alan suddenly became aware that Francis Garvey was really worried. The youngster's face was twisted into an unhappy mixture of bashfulness and uncertainty.

Alan stared at him in astonishment. "You're not *scared* are you?"

Garvey gestured vaguely with one hand. "I'm not scared. It's just"—the words came out with an effort—"I've never done this before."

Alan said, "Well I'll be damned." He took Garvey by the arm and started to walk him across the room, talking almost to himself. "This is one for the books. The guy who cracked the fear generator is afraid to talk to a girl. Boy, that mission *really* cleaned you out. If you'd tried to fly another one, you'd have been a dead pigeon."

Alan stopped walking, with a strange look on his face. When the youth's arm tugged him, he went on again, his eyes slightly glassy.

Neither Garvey nor Marilyn noticed how absent-mindedly Alan introduced them. Nor did they notice when he strolled away muttering to himself, the strange expression still on his face.

Five minutes later, when Dr. Murchison came over to congratulate him for the fourth time, Alan was staring at his hands as though he had just discovered them. His hands were trembling violently.

Murchison started to speak, then stopped and scowled at Alan. "You look pale," he said. "Here, have my drink."

Alan recognized him with a start. "I look funny? Funny. Y'know what just dawned on me, Murch? Garvey was only good for one mission. If he hadn't found the answer on that one mission, *we'd have had it.*"

Murchison looked relieved. "Of course. I knew that the minute I saw him when he came back.

"Yes, but the only way he found it was that he recognized it felt like the Screep. What if I hadn't tried to Screep him?"

Thoughtfully, Murchison said, "Gimme back my drink."

Alan chuckled. "Now to make this party complete. I've got to make an important call." He headed for the PV in the director's office.

Ann Fitzgerald wasn't the kind of person who could pretend too long. She'd been more wretched than angry for some time. They hadn't seen each other since the violence of their last meeting and parting lay like a pall between them. They didn't quite meet each other's eyes.

"Ann, dear," he said, soberly, and a little abashed. "It looks like we've beaten this thing and we're kind of celebrating over here. I...was wondering if you'd care to come over and share it with me."

She hesitated awkwardly for a moment, then smiled her gladness. "Sure, Alan, I'd love to."

"Gee, Ann, that's wonderful." His face lit up. "I'll be over to pick you up right away." He blew her a kiss; reached for the switch, and remembered something. "Oh, Ann...I'll have someone with me. Will you mind?"

She looked puzzled, and a little of the stiffness came back into her face. "No, of course not, Alan."

Alan pried Francis Garvey from Marilyn, promising he'd have him back in half an hour. They went over in a helicar borrowed from one of the professors. Garvey wanted to wait in the car, but Alan pushed him up the stairs, and stood behind him as he rang the bell.

Ann opened the door and started to greet Alan. Then she stared at Francis Garvey—almost recognized him. He was looking at her with a sort of wary friendliness.

She looked puzzled as she tried to place him—confused by his uniform—then went wide-eyed as she remembered. Her fingers came up to her mouth, and a flush spread over her shoulders and throat, mounting to her cheeks.

Alan stepped forward and said, "Ann, this is Francis Garvey. Francis, Ann Fitzgerald."

Garvey said, "Pleased to meet you, Miss Fitzgerald. Please accept my apology for the last time we met."

Ann stammered and her eyes grew very wide. The three stared at each other for a moment, until Alan broke the silence. Quietly he explained to Ann the part Garvey had played in their success—the changes it had accomplished in him—and what it would mean for others like him.

Ann listened, the color subsiding from her face. But she

was nodding quietly when Alan finished. And when Kerr asked Garvey if he'd mind waiting a minute or two back in the helicar for them, Ann shook Garvey's hand impulsively, and wished him the best of luck.

As soon as Garvey had disappeared around the landing, she threw herself into Alan's arms, and buried her face in his shoulder. When he lifted her chin, to kiss her, she was smiling through her tears.

"How are you darling," she said. "Just stand still and let me admire you. I've never seen you looking quite so young and handsome."

"Can't stand still," he said. "Not at the moment. Even if you threw yourself in my arms I couldn't manage it."

"Why not, darling?"

"Can't you see why not? I'm two-way intoxicated."

"Just what do you mean by that?"

"Well, I must have had at least ten Scotch highballs. But you're the one who really intoxicates me. Just take hold of my arm and we'll walk slowly back to Garvey and the helicar—and make the party a complete success."

"Suits me," she said, smiling happily, taking very firm hold of his arm.

They started walking down the stairs, their arms very tightly interlinked.

Alan muttered to himself, "Oh, what a wise old psychologist am I—and what one hell of a party it'll be."

It was.

THE END

If you've enjoyed this book, you will not want to miss these terrific titles…

ARMCHAIR SCI-FI & HORROR DOUBLE NOVELS, $12.95 each

D-21   **EMPIRE OF EVIL** by Robert Arnette
THE SIGN OF THE TIGER by Alan E. Nourse & J. A. Meyer

D-22   **OPERATION SQUARE PEG** by Frank Belknap Long
ENCHANTRESS OF VENUS by Leigh Brackett

D-23   **THE LIFE WATCH** by Lester Del Rey
CREATURES OF THE ABYSS by Murray Leinster

D-24   **BLACK MAGIC HOLIDAY** by Robert Bloch
STAR HUNTER by Andre Norton

D-25   **EMPIRE OF WOMEN** by John Fletcher
ONE OF OUR CITIES IS MISSING by Irving Cox

D-26   **THE WRONG SIDE OF PARADISE** by Raymond F. Jones
THE INVOLUNTARY IMMORTALS by Rog Phillips

D-27   **EARTH QUARTER** by Damon Knight
ENVOY TO NEW WORLDS by Keith Laumer

D-28   **SLAVES TO THE METAL HORDE** by Milton Lesser
HUNTERS OUT OF TIME by Joseph E. Kelleam

D-29   **RX JUPITER SAVE US** by Ward Moore
BEWARE THE USURPERS by Geoff St. Reynard

D-30   **SECRET OF THE SERPENT** by Don Wilcox
CRUSADE ACROSS THE VOID by Dwight V. Swain

ARMCHAIR SCIENCE FICTION CLASSICS, $12.95 each

C-7   **THE SHAVER MYSTERY, pt. 1**
by Richard S. Shaver

C-8   **THE SHAVER MYSTERY, pt. 2**
by Richard S. Shaver

C-9   **MURDER IN SPACE** by David V. Reed
by David V. Reed

ARMCHAIR MASTERS OF SCIENCE FICTION SERIES, $16.95 each

M-3   **MASTERS OF SCIENCE FICTION, Vol. Three**
Robert Sheckley

M-4   **MASTERS OF SCIENCE FICTION, Vol. Four**
Mack Reynolds, part one

A THRILLING NOVEL OF THE LOST ONES

Laughing, she cast him down into the hideous depths, beneath the seas of flaming gas, to where dead blossoms swayed, whispering, over strangely jumbled ruins…

But there he found the secret of her power, and came surging back—up from the depths, from the seas, the tortured swamps—to storm her forbidden temple and seek her within, death like a gift in his hand!

Joined famed science fiction author Leigh Brackett as she spins a tale of outer space adventure and intrigue, direct from the pages of Planet Stories *magazine.*

CAST OF CHARACTERS

STARK

He was a man who had been around the Universe, and he had come to Venus to rescue a friend who had once saved his life.

HELVI

He had mysteriously disappeared into the Shuruun and never returned. Stark knew he must find him.

VARRA

This she devil was someone you didn't want to cross, especially with a killer falcon and a two-headed dragon at her disposal.

MIKE LARRABEE

He was one of only a few Earthmen on the planet Venus. But was he friend…or foe?

MALTHOR

This Venusian ship captain had more in mind than just collecting passenger fares.

ZARETH

She was Malthor's daughter, but when she befriended a man from another planet it cost her dearly.

THE LHARI

These elite, god-like creatures felt no mercy or emotion other than pleasing themselves.

ENCHANTRESS
OF VENUS

By
LEIGH BRACKETT

ARMCHAIR FICTION
PO Box 4369, Medford, Oregon 97504

CHAPTER ONE

THE SHIP MOVED SLOWLY across the Red Sea, through the shrouding veils of mist, her sail barely filled by the languid thrust of the wind. Her hull, of a thin light metal, floated without sound, the surface of the strange ocean parting before her prow in silent rippling streamers of flame.

Night deepened toward the ship, a river of indigo flowing out of the west. The man known as Stark stood alone by the after rail and watched its coming. He was full of impatience and a gathering sense of danger, so that it seemed to him that even the hot wind smelled of it.

The steersman lay drowsily over his sweep. He was a big man, with skin and hair the color of milk. He did not speak, but Stark felt that now and again the man's eyes turned toward him, pale and calculating under half-closed lids, with a secret avarice.

The captain and the two other members of the little coasting vessel's crew were forward, at their evening meal. Once or twice Stark heard a burst of laughter, half-whispered and furtive. It was as though all four shared in some private joke, from which he was rigidly excluded.

The heat was oppressive. Sweat gathered on Stark's dark face. His shirt stuck to his back. The air was heavy with moisture, tainted with the muddy fecundity of the land that brooded westward behind the eternal fog.

There was something ominous about the sea itself. Even on its own world, the Red Sea is hardly more than legend. It lies behind the Mountains of White Cloud, the great barrier wall that hides away half a planet. Few men have gone beyond that barrier, into the vast mystery of Inner Venus. Fewer still have come back.

Enchantress Of Venus

By LEIGH BRACKETT

Stark was one of that handful. Three times before he had crossed the mountains, and once he had stayed for nearly a year. But he had never quite grown used to the Red Sea.

It was not water. It was gaseous, dense enough to float the buoyant hulls of the metal ships, and it burned perpetually with its deep inner fires. The mists that clouded it were stained with the bloody glow. Beneath the surface Stark could see the drifts of flame where the lazy currents ran, and the little coiling bursts of sparks that came upward and spread and melted into other bursts, so that the face of the sea was like a cosmos of crimson stars.

It was very beautiful, glowing against the blue, luminous darkness of the night. Beautiful, and strange.

There was a padding of bare feet, and the captain, Malthor,

There was a great boiling roar—the slaves were attacking!

Laughing, she cast him down into the hideous depths, beneath the seas of flaming gas, to where dead blossoms swayed, whispering, over strangely jumbled ruins . . . But there he found the secret of her power, and came surging back—up from the depths, up from the seas, the tortured swamps—to storm her forbidding shrine and seek her within, death like a gift in his hands . . .

133

came up to Stark, his outlines dim and ghostly in the gloom.

"We will reach Shuruun," he said, "before the second glass is run."

Stark nodded. "Good."

The voyage had seemed endless, and the close confinement of the narrow deck had got badly on his nerves.

"You will like Shuruun," said the captain jovially. "Our wine, our food, our women—all superb. We don't have many visitors. We keep to ourselves, as you will see. But those who do come…"

He laughed, and clapped Stark on the shoulder. "Ah, yes. You will be happy in Shuruun."

It seemed to Stark that he caught an echo of laughter from the unseen crew, as though they listened and found a hidden jest in Malthor's words.

Stark said, "That's fine."

"Perhaps," said Malthor, "you would like to lodge with me, I could make you a good price."

He had made a good price for Stark's passage from up the coast. An exorbitantly good one.

Stark said, "No."

"You don't have to be afraid," said the Venusian, in a confidential tone. "The strangers who come to Shuruun all have the same reason. It's a good place to hide. We're out of everybody's reach."

He paused, but Stark did not rise to his bait. Presently he chuckled and went on, "In fact, it's such a safe place that most of the strangers decide to stay on. Now, at my house, I could give you…"

Stark said again, flatly, "No."

The captain shrugged. "Very well. Think it over, anyway." He peered ahead into the red, coiling mists. "Ah…see there?" He pointed, and Stark made out the shadowy loom of cliffs. "We are coming into the strait now."

Malthor turned and took the steering sweep himself, the helmsman going forward to join the others. The ship began to pick up speed. Stark saw that she had come into the grip of a current that swept toward the cliffs, a river of fire racing ever more swiftly in the depths of the sea.

THE dark wall seemed to plunge toward them. At first Stark could see no passage. Then, suddenly, a narrow crimson streak appeared, widened, and became a gut of boiling flame, rushing silently around broken rocks. Red fog rose like smoke. The ship quivered, sprang ahead, and tore like a mad thing into the heart of the inferno.

In spite of himself, Stark's hands tightened on the rail. Tattered veils of mist swirled past them. The sea, the air, the ship itself, seemed drenched in blood. There was no sound, in all that wild sweep of current through the strait. Only the sullen fires burst and flowed.

The reflected glare showed Stark that the Straits of Shuruun were defended. Squat fortresses brooded on the cliffs. There were ballistas and great windlasses for the drawing of nets across the narrow throat. The men of Shuruun could enforce their law that barred all foreign shipping from their gulf.

They had reason for such a law, and such a defense. The legitimate trade of Shuruun, such as it was, was in wine and the delicate laces woven from spider-silk. Actually, however, the city lived and throve on piracy, the arts of wrecking and contraband trade in the distilled juice of the *vela* poppy.

Looking at the rocks and the fortresses, Stark could understand how it was that Shuruun had been able for more centuries than anyone could tell to victimize the shipping of the Red Sea, and offer a refuge to the outlaw, the wolf's-head, the breaker of tabu.

With startling abruptness, they were through the gut and

drifting on the still surface of this all but landlocked arm of the Red Sea.

Because of the shrouding fog, Stark could see nothing of the land. But the smell of it was stronger, warm damp soil and the heavy, faintly rotten perfume of vegetation half jungle, half swamp. Once, through a rift in the wreathing vapor, he thought he glimpsed the shadowy bulk of an island, but it was gone at once.

After the terrifying rush of the strait, it seemed to Stark that the ship barely moved. His impatience and the subtle sense of danger deepened. He began to pace the deck, with the nervous, velvet motion of a prowling cat. The moist, steamy air seemed all but unbreathable after the clean dryness of Mars, from whence he had come so recently. It was oppressively still.

Suddenly he stopped, his head thrown back, listening.

The sound was borne faintly on the slow wind. It came from everywhere and nowhere, a vague dim thing without source or direction. It almost seemed that the night itself had spoken—the hot blue night of Venus, crying out of the mists with a tongue of infinite woe.

It faded and died away, only half heard, leaving behind it a sense of aching sadness, as though all the misery and longing of a world had found voice in that desolate wail.

Stark shivered. For a time there was silence, and then he heard the sound again, now on a deeper note. Still faint and far away, it was sustained longer by the vagaries of the heavy air, and it became a chant, rising and falling. There were no words. It was not the sort of thing that would have need of words. Then it was gone again.

Stark turned to Malthor. "What was that?"

The man looked at him curiously. He seemed not to have heard.

"That wailing sound," said Stark impatiently.

"Oh, that." The Venusian shrugged. "A trick of the wind. It sighs in the hollow rocks around the strait."

HE YAWNED, giving place again to the steersman, and came to stand beside Stark. The Earthman ignored him. For some reason, that sound half heard through the mists had brought his uneasiness to a sharp pitch.

Civilization had brushed over Stark with a light hand. Raised from infancy by half-human aboriginals, his perceptions were still those of a savage. His ear was good.

Malthor lied. That cry of pain was not made by any wind.

"I've known several Earthmen," said Malthor changing the subject, but not too swiftly. "None of them were like you."

Intuition warned Stark to play along. "I don't come from Earth," he said. "I come from Mercury."

Malthor puzzled over that. Venus is a cloudy world, where no man has ever seen the Sun, let alone a star. The captain had heard vaguely of these things. Earth and Mars he knew of. But Mercury was an unknown word.

Stark explained. "The planet nearest the Sun. It's very hot there. The Sun blazes like a huge fire, and there are no clouds to shield it."

"Ah. That is why your skin is so dark." He held his own pale forearm close to Stark's and shook his head. "I have never seen such skin," he said admiringly. "Nor such great muscles."

Looking up, he went on in a tone of complete friendliness, "I wish you would stay with me. You'll find no better lodgings in Shuruun. And I warn you, there are people in the town who will take advantage of strangers—rob them, even slay them. Now, I am known by all as a man of honour. You could sleep soundly under my roof."

He paused, then added with a smile, "Also, I have a

daughter. An excellent cook—and very beautiful."

The woeful chanting came again, dim and distant on the wind, an echo of warning against some unimagined fate.

Stark said for the third time, "No."

He needed no intuition to tell him to walk wide of the captain. The man was a rogue, and not a very subtle one.

A flint-hard, angry look came briefly into Malthor's eyes. "You're a stubborn man. You'll find that Shuruun is no place for stubbornness."

He turned and went away. Stark remained where he was. The ship drifted on through a slow eternity of time. And all down that long still gulf of the Red Sea, through the heat and the wreathing fog, the ghostly chanting haunted him, like the keening of lost souls in some forgotten hell.

Presently the course of the ship was altered. Malthor came again to the afterdeck, giving a few quiet commands. Stark saw land ahead, a darker blur on the night, and then the shrouded outlines of a city.

Torches blazed on the quays and in the streets, and the low buildings caught a ruddy glow from the burning sea itself. A squat and ugly town, Shuruun, crouching witch-like on the rocky shore, her ragged skirts dipped in blood.

The ship drifted in toward the quays.

STARK heard a whisper of movement behind him, the hushed and purposeful padding of naked feet. He turned, with the astonishing swiftness of an animal that feels itself threatened, his hand dropping to his gun.

A belaying pin, thrown by the steersman, struck the side of his head with stunning force. Reeling, half-blinded, he saw the distorted shapes of men closing in upon him. Malthor's voice sounded, low and hard. A second belaying pin whizzed through the air and cracked against Stark's shoulder.

Hands were laid upon him. Bodies, heavy and strong,

bore his down. Malthor laughed.

Stark's teeth glinted bare and white. Someone's cheek brushed past, and he sank them into the flesh. He began to growl a sound that should never have come from a human throat. It seemed to the startled Venusians that the man they had attacked had by some wizardry become a beast, at the first touch of violence.

The man with the torn cheek screamed. There was a voiceless scuffling on the deck, a terrible intensity of motion, and then the great dark body rose and shook itself free of the tangle, and was gone, over the rail, leaving Malthor with nothing but the silken rags of a shirt in his hands.

The surface of the Red Sea closed without a ripple over Stark. There was a burst of crimson sparks, a momentary trail of flame going down like a drowned comet, and then—nothing.

CHAPTER TWO

STARK dropped slowly downward through a strange world. There was no difficulty about breathing, as in a sea of water. The gases of the Red Sea support life quite well, and the creatures that dwell in it have almost normal lungs.

Stark did not pay much attention at first, except to keep his balance automatically. He was still dazed from the blow, and he was raging with anger and pain.

The primitive in him, whose name was not Stark but N'Chaka, and who had fought and starved and hunted in the blazing valleys of Mercury's Twilight Belt, learning lessons he never forgot, wished to return and slay Malthor and his men. He regretted that he had not torn out their throats, for now his trail would never be safe from them.

But the man Stark, who had learned some more bitter lessons in the name of civilization, knew the unwisdom of that. He snarled over his aching head, and cursed the Venusians in the harsh, crude dialect that was his mother tongue, but he did not turn back. There would be time enough for Malthor.

It struck him that the gulf was very deep.

Fighting down his rage, he began to swim in the direction of the shore. There was no sign of pursuit, and he judged that Malthor had decided to let him go. He puzzled over the reason for the attack. It could hardly be robbery, since he carried nothing but the clothes he stood in, and very little money.

No. There was some deeper reason. A reason connected with Malthor's insistence that he lodge with him. Stark smiled. It was not a pleasant smile. He was thinking of Shuruun, and the things men said about it, around the shores of the Red Sea.

Then his face hardened. The dim coiling fires through which he swam brought him memories of other times he had gone adventuring in the depths of the Red Sea.

He had not been alone then. Helvi had gone with him— the tall son of a barbarian kinglet up-coast by Yarell. They had hunted strange beasts through the crystal forests of the sea-bottom and bathed in the welling flames that pulse from the very heart of Venus to feed the ocean. They had been brothers.

Now Helvi was gone, into Shuruun. He had never returned.

Stark swam on. And presently he saw below him in the red gloom something that made him drop lower, frowning with surprise.

There were trees beneath him. Great forest giants, towering up into an eerie sky, their branches swaying gently to the slow wash of the currents.

Stark was puzzled. The forests where he and Helvi had

hunted were truly crystalline, without even the memory of life. The "trees" were no more trees in actuality than the branching corals of Terra's southern oceans.

But these were real, or had been. He thought at first that they still lived, for their leaves were green, and here and there creepers had starred them with great nodding blossoms of gold and purple and waxy white. But when he floated down close enough to touch them, he realized that they were dead—trees, creepers, blossoms, all.

They had not mummified, nor turned to stone. They were pliable, and their colors were very bright. Simply, they had ceased to live, and the gases of the sea had preserved them by some chemical magic, so perfectly that barely a leaf had fallen.

Stark did not venture into the shadowy denseness below the topmost branches. A strange fear came over him, at the sight of that vast forest dreaming in the depths of the gulf, drowned and forgotten, as though wondering why the birds had gone, taking with them the warm rains and the light of day.

He thrust his way upward, himself like a huge dark bird above the branches. An overwhelming impulse to get away from that unearthly place drove him on, his half-wild sense shuddering with an impression of evil so great that it took all his acquired common-sense to assure him that he was not pursued by demons.

HE BROKE the surface at last, to find that he had lost his direction in the red deep and made a long circle around, so that he was far below Shuruun. He made his way back, not hurrying now, and presently clambered out over the black rocks.

He stood at the end of a muddy lane that wandered in toward the town. He followed it, moving neither fast nor slow, but with a wary alertness.

Huts of wattle-and-daub took shape out of the fog, increased in numbers, became a street of dwellings. Here and there rush-lights glimmered through the slitted windows. A man and a woman clung together in a low doorway. They saw him and sprang apart, and the woman gave a little cry. Stark went on. He did not look back, but he knew that they were following him quietly, at a little distance.

The lane twisted snakelike upon itself, crawling now through a crowded jumble of houses. There were more lights, and more people, tall white-skinned folk of the swamp edges, with pale eyes and long hair the colour of new flax, and the faces of wolves.

Stark passed among them, alien and strange with his black hair and sun-darkened skin. They did not speak, nor try to stop him. Only they looked at him out of the red fog, with a curious blend of amusement and fear, and some of them followed him, keeping well behind. A gang of small naked children came from somewhere among the houses and ran shouting beside him, out of reach, until one boy threw a stone and screamed something unintelligible except for one word—*Lhari.* Then they all stopped, horrified, and fled.

Stark went on, through the quarter of the lacemakers, heading by instinct toward the wharves. The glow of the Red Sea pervaded all the air, so that it seemed as though the mist was full of tiny drops of blood. There was a smell about the place he did not like, a damp miasma of mud and crowding bodies and wine, and the breath of the *vela* poppy. Shuruun was an unclean town, and it stank of evil.

There was something else about it, a subtle thing that touched Stark's nerves with a chill finger. Fear. He could see the shadow of it in the eyes of the people, hear its undertone in their voices. The wolves of Shuruun did not feel safe in their own kennel. Unconsciously, as this feeling grew upon him, Stark's step grew more and more wary, his eyes more cold and hard.

He came out into a broad square by the harbor front. He could see the ghostly ships moored along the quays, the piled casks of wine, the tangle of masts and cordage dim against the background of the burning gulf. There were many torches here. Large low buildings stood around the square. There was laughter and the sound of voices from the dark verandas, and somewhere a woman sang to the melancholy lilting of a reed pipe.

A suffused glow of light in the distance ahead caught Stark's eye. That way the streets sloped to a higher ground, and straining his vision against the fog, he made out very dimly the tall bulk of a castle crouched on the low cliffs, looking with bright eyes upon the night, and the streets of Shuruun.

Stark hesitated briefly. Then he started across the square toward the largest of the taverns.

There were a number of people in the open space, mostly sailors and their women. They were loose and foolish with wine, but even so they stopped where they were and stared at the dark stranger, and then drew back from him, still staring.

Those who had followed Stark came into the square after him and then paused, spreading out in an aimless sort of way to join with other groups, whispering among themselves.

The woman stopped singing in the middle of a phrase.

A curious silence fell on the square. A nervous sibilance ran round and round under the silence, and men came slowly out from the verandas and the doors of the wine shops. Suddenly a woman with disheveled hair pointed her arm at Stark and laughed the shrieking laugh of a harpy.

STARK found his way barred by three tall young men with hard mouths and crafty eyes, who smiled at him as hound's smile before the kill.

"Stranger," they said. "Earthman."

"Outlaw," answered Stark, and it was only half a lie.

One of the young men took a step forward. "Did you fly like a dragon over the Mountains of White Cloud? Did you drop from the sky?"

"I came on Malthor's ship."

A kind of sigh went round the square and with it the name of Malthor. The eager faces of the young men grew heavy with disappointment. But the leader said sharply, "I was on the quay when Malthor docked. You were not on board."

It was Stark's turn to smile. In the light of the torches, his eyes blazed cold and bright as ice against the sun.

"Ask Malthor the reason for that," he said. "Ask the man with the torn cheek. Or perhaps," he added softly, "you would like to learn for yourselves."

The young men looked at him, scowling, in an odd mood of indecision. Stark settled himself, every muscle loose and ready. And the woman who had laughed crept closer and peered at Stark through her tangled hair, breathing heavily of the poppy wine.

All at once she said loudly, "He came out of the sea. That's where he came from. He's…"

One of the young men struck her across the mouth and she fell down in the mud. A burly seaman ran out and caught her by the hair, dragging her to her feet again. His face was frightened and very angry. He hauled the woman away, cursing her for a fool and beating her as he went. She spat out blood, and said no more.

"Well," said Stark to the young men. "Have you made up your minds?"

"Minds!" said a voice behind them—a harsh-timbered, rasping voice that handled the liquid vocables of the Venusian speech very clumsily indeed. "They have no minds, these whelps! If they had, they'd be off about their business, instead of standing here badgering a stranger."

The young men turned, and now between them Stark could see the man who had spoken. He stood on the steps of the tavern. He was an Earthman, and at first Stark thought he was old, because his hair was white and his face deeply lined. His body was wasted with fever, the muscles all gone to knotty strings twisted over bone. He leaned heavily on a stick, and one leg was crooked and terribly scarred.

He grinned at Stark and said, in colloquial English, "Watch me get rid of 'em!"

He began to tongue-lash the young men, telling them that they were idiots, the misbegotten offspring of swamp-toads, utterly without manners, and that if they did not believe the stranger's story they should go and ask Malthor, as he suggested. Finally he shook his stick at them, fairly screeching.

"Go on, now. Go away! Leave us alone—my brother of Earth and I."

The young men gave one hesitant glance at Stark's feral eyes. Then they looked at each other and shrugged, and went away across the square half sheepishly, like great loutish boys caught in some misdemeanor.

The white-haired Earthman beckoned to Stark. And, as Stark came up to him on the steps he said under his breath, almost angrily, "You're in a trap."

Stark glanced back over his shoulder. At the edge of the square the three young men had met a fourth, who had his face bound up in a rag. They vanished almost at once into a side street, but not before Stark had recognized the fourth man as Malthor.

It was the captain he had branded.

With loud cheerfulness, the lame man said in Venusian, "Come in and drink with me, brother, and we will talk of Earth."

CHAPTER THREE

THE TAVERN WAS OF THE standard low-class Venusian pattern—a single huge room under bare thatch, the wall half open with the reed shutters rolled up, the floor of split logs propped up on piling out of the mud. A long low bar, little tables, mangy skins and heaps of dubious cushions on the floor around them, and at one end the entertainers—two old men with a drum and a reed pipe, and a couple of sulky, tired-looking girls.

The lame man led Stark to a table in the corner and sank down, calling for wine. His eyes, which were dark and haunted by long pain, burned with excitement. His hands shook. Before Stark had sat down he had begun to talk, his words stumbling over themselves as though he could not get them out fast enough.

"How is it there now? Has it changed any? Tell me how it is—the cities, the lights, the paved streets, the women, the Sun. Oh Lord, what I wouldn't give to see the Sun again, and women with dark hair and their clothes on." He leaned forward, staring hungrily into Stark's face, as though he could see those things mirrored there. "For God's sake, talk to me—talk to me in English, and tell me about Earth!"

"How long have you been here?" asked Stark.

"I don't know. How do you reckon time on a world without a Sun, without one damned little star to look at? Ten years, a hundred years, how should I know? Forever. Tell me about Earth."

Stark smiled wryly. "I haven't been there for a long time. The police were too ready with a welcoming committee. But the last time I saw it, it was just the same."

The lame man shivered. He was not looking at Stark now, but at some place far beyond him.

"Autumn woods," he said. "Red and gold on the brown hills. Snow. I can remember how it felt to be cold. The air bit you when you breathed it. And the women wore high-heeled slippers. No big bare feet tromping in the mud, but little sharp heels tapping on clean pavement."

Suddenly he glared at Stark, his eyes furious and bright with tears.

"Why the hell did you have to come here and start me remembering? I'm Larrabee. I live in Shuruun. I've been here forever, and I'll be here till I die. There isn't any Earth. It's gone. Just look up into the sky, and you'll know it's gone. There's nothing anywhere but clouds, and Venus, and mud."

He sat still, shaking, turning his head from side to side. A man came with wine, put it down, and went away again. The tavern was very quiet. There was a wide space empty around the two Earthmen. Beyond that people lay on the cushions, sipping the poppy wine and watching with a sort of furtive expectancy.

Abruptly, Larrabee laughed, a harsh sound that held a certain honest mirth.

"I don't know why I should get sentimental about Earth at this late date. Never thought much about it when I was there."

Nevertheless, he kept his gaze averted, and when he picked up his cup his hand trembled so that he spilled some of the wine.

Stark was staring at him in unbelief. "Larrabee," he said. "You're Mike Larrabee. You're the man who got half a million credits out of the strong room of the *Royal Venus*."

Larrabee nodded. "And got away with it, right over the Mountains of White Cloud, that they said couldn't be flown. And do you know where that half a million is now? At the bottom of the Red Sea, along with my ship and my crew, out there in the gulf. Lord knows why I lived." He shrugged.

"Well, anyway, I was heading for Shuruun when I crashed, and I got here. So why complain?"

He drank again, deeply, and Stark shook his head.

"You've been here nine years, then, by Earth time," he said. He had never met Larrabee, but he remembered the pictures of him that had flashed across space on police bands. Larrabee had been a young man then, dark and proud and handsome.

Larrabee guessed his thought. "I've changed, haven't I?"

Stark said lamely, "Everybody thought you were dead."

LARRABEE laughed. After that, for a moment, there was silence. Stark's ears were straining for any sound outside. There was none.

He said abruptly, "What about this trap I'm in?"

"I'll tell you one thing about it," said Larrabee. "There's no way out. I can't help you. I wouldn't if I could, get that straight. But I can't, anyway."

"Thanks," Stark said sourly. "You can at least tell me what goes on."

"Listen," said Larrabee. "I'm a cripple, and an old man, and Shuruun isn't the sweetest place in the Solar System to live. But I do live. I have a wife, a slatternly wench I'll admit, but good enough in her way. You'll notice some little dark-haired brats rolling in the mud. They're mine, too. I have some skill at setting bones and such, and so I can get drunk for nothing as often as I will—which is often. Also, because of this bum leg, I'm perfectly safe. So don't ask me what goes on. I take great pains not to know."

Stark said, "Who are the Lhari?"

"Would you like to meet them?" Larrabee seemed to find something very amusing in that thought. "Just go on up to the castle. They live there. They're the Lords of Shuruun, and they're always glad to meet strangers."

He leaned forward suddenly. "Who are you anyway? What's your name, and why the devil did you come here?"

"My name is Stark. And I came here for the same reason you did."

"Stark," repeated Larrabee slowly, his eyes intent. "That rings a faint bell. Seems to me I saw a *Wanted* flash once, some idiot that had led a native revolt somewhere in the Jovian Colonies—a big cold-eyed brute they referred to colorfully as the wild man from Mercury."

He nodded, pleased with himself. "Wild man, eh? Well, Shuruun will tame you down."

"Perhaps," said Stark. His eyes shifted rapidly, watching Larrabee, watching the doorway, and the dark veranda and the people who drank but did not talk among themselves. "Speaking of strangers, one came here at the time of the last rains. He was Venusian, from up coast. A big young man. I used to know him. Perhaps he could help me."

Larrabee snorted. By now, he had drunk his own wine and Stark's too. "Nobody can help you. As for your friend, I never saw him. I'm beginning to think I should never have seen you." Quite suddenly he caught up his stick and got with some difficulty to his feet. He did not look at Stark, but said harshly, "You better get out of here." Then he turned and limped unsteadily to the bar.

Stark rose. He glanced after Larrabee, and again his nostrils twitched to the smell of fear. Then he went out of the tavern the way he had come in, through the front door. No one moved to stop him. Outside, the square was empty. It had begun to rain.

Stark stood for a moment on the steps. He was angry, and filled with a dangerous unease, the hair-trigger nervousness of a tiger that senses the beaters creeping toward him up the wind. He would almost have welcomed the sight of Malthor and the three young men. But there was nothing to fight but the silence and the rain.

HE STEPPED out into the mud, wet and warm around his ankles. An idea came to him, and he smiled, beginning now to move with a definite purpose, along the side of the square.

The sharp downpour strengthened. Rain smoked from Stark's naked shoulders, beat against thatch and mud with a hissing rattle. The harbor had disappeared behind boiling clouds of fog, where water struck the surface of the Red Sea and was turned again instantly by chemical action into vapor. The quays and the neighboring streets were being swallowed up in the impenetrable mist. Lightning came with an eerie bluish flare, and thunder came rolling after it.

Stark turned up the narrow way that led toward the castle.

Its lights were winking out now, one by one, blotted by the creeping fog. Lightning etched its shadowy bulk against the night, and then was gone. And through the noise of the thunder that followed, Stark thought he heard a voice calling.

He stopped, half crouching, his hand on his gun. The cry came again, a girl's voice, thin as the wail of a sea bird through the driving rain. Then he saw her, a small white blur in the street behind him, running, and even in that dim glimpse of her, every line of her body was instinct with fright.

Stark set his back against a wall and waited. There did not seem to be anyone with her, though it was hard to tell in the darkness and the storm.

She came up to him, and stopped, just out of his reach, looking at him and away again with a painful irresoluteness. A bright flash showed her to him clearly. She was young, not long out of her childhood, and pretty in a stupid sort of way. Just now her mouth trembled on the edge of weeping, and her eyes were very large and scared. Her skirt clung to her long thighs, and above it her naked body, hardly fleshed into womanhood, glistened like snow in the wet. Her pale hair hung dripping over her shoulders.

Stark said gently, "What do you want with me?"

She looked at him, so miserably like a wet puppy that he smiled. And as though that smile had taken what little resolution she had out of her, she dropped to her knees, sobbing.

"I can't do it," she wailed. "He'll kill me, but I just can't do it!"

"Do what?" asked Stark.

She stared up at him. "Run away," she urged him. "Run away now. You'll die in the swamps, but that's better than being one of the Lost Ones." She shook her thin arms at him. "Run away!"

CHAPTER FOUR

THE STREET WAS EMPTY. Nothing showed, nothing stirred anywhere. Stark leaned over and pulled the girl to her feet, drawing her in under the shelter of the thatched eaves.

"Now then," he said. "Suppose you stop crying and tell me what this is all about."

Presently, between gulps and hiccups, he got the story out of her.

"I am Zareth," she said. "Malthor's daughter. He's afraid of you, because of what you did to him on the ship, so he ordered me to watch for you in the square, when you would come out of the tavern. Then I was to follow you, and…"

She broke off, and Stark patted her shoulder. "Go on."

But a new thought had occurred to her. "If I do, will you promise not to beat me, or…" She looked at his gun and shivered.

"I promise."

She studied his face, what she could see of it in the

darkness, and then seemed to lose some of her fear.

"I was to stop you. I was to say what I've already said, about being Malthor's daughter and the rest of it, and then I was to say that he wanted me to lead you into an ambush while pretending to help you escape, but that I couldn't do it, and would help you to escape anyhow because I hated Malthor and the whole business about the Lost Ones. So you would believe me, and follow me, and I would lead you into the ambush."

She shook her head and began to cry again, quietly this time, and there was nothing of the woman about her at all now. She was just a child, very miserable and afraid. Stark was glad he had branded Malthor.

"But I can't lead you into the ambush. I do hate Malthor, even if he is my father, because he beats me. And the Lost Ones..." She paused. "Sometimes I hear them at night, chanting way out there beyond the mist. It is a very terrible sound."

"It is," said Stark. "I've heard it. Who are the Lost Ones, Zareth?"

"I can't tell you that," said Zareth. "It's forbidden even to speak of them. And anyway," she finished honestly, "I don't even know. People disappear, that's all. Not our own people of Shuruun, at least not very often. But strangers like you— and I'm sure my father goes off into the swamps to hunt among the tribes there, and I'm sure he comes back from some of his voyages with nothing in his hold but men from some captured ship. Why, or what for, I don't know. Except I've heard the chanting."

"They live out there in the gulf, do they, the Lost Ones?"

"They must. There are many islands there."

"And what of the Lhari, the Lords of Shuruun? Don't they know what's going on? Or are they part of it?"

She shuddered, and said, "It's not for us to question the

Lhari, nor even to wonder what they do. Those who have are gone from Shuruun, nobody knows where."

Stark nodded. He was silent for a moment, thinking. Then Zareth's little hand touched his shoulder.

"Go," she said. "Lose yourself in the swamps. You're strong, and there's something about you different from other men. You may live to find your way through."

"No. I have something to do before I leave Shuruun." He took Zareth's damp fair head between his hands and kissed her on the forehead. "You're a sweet child, Zareth, and a brave one. Tell Malthor that you did exactly as he told you, and it was not your fault I wouldn't follow you."

"He will beat me anyway," said Zareth philosophically, "but perhaps not quite so hard."

"He'll have no reason to beat you at all, if you tell him the truth—that I would not go with you because my mind was set on going to the castle of the Lhari."

THERE was a long, long silence, while Zareth's eyes widened slowly in horror, and the rain beat on the thatch, and fog and thunder rolled together across Shuruun.

"To the castle," she whispered. "Oh, no! Go into the swamps, or let Malthor take you—but don't go to the castle!" She took hold of his arm, her fingers biting into his flesh with the urgency of her plea. "You're a stranger, you don't know...please, don't go up there."

"Why not?" asked Stark. "Are the Lhari demons? Do they devour men?" He loosened her hands gently. "You'd better go now. Tell your father where I am, if he wishes to come after me."

Zareth backed away slowly, out into the rain, staring at him as though she looked at someone standing on the brink of hell, not dead, but worse than dead. Wonder showed in her face, and through it a great yearning pity. She tried once

153

to speak, and then shook her head and turned away, breaking into a run as though she could not endure to look upon Stark any longer. In a second she was gone.

Stark looked after her for a moment, strangely touched. Then he stepped out into the rain again, heading upward along the steep path that led to the castle of the Lords of Shuruun.

The mist was blinding. Stark had to feel his way, and as he climbed higher, above the level of the town, he was lost in the sullen redness. A hot wind blew, and each flare of lighting turned the crimson fog to a hellish purple. The night was full of a vast hissing where the rain poured into the gulf. He stopped once to hide his gun in a cleft between the rocks.

At length he stumbled against a carven pillar of black stone and found the gate that hung from it, a massive thing sheathed in metal. It was barred, and the pounding of his fists upon it made little sound.

Then he saw the gong, a huge disc of beaten gold beside the gate. Stark picked up the hammer that lay there, and set the deep voice of the gong rolling out between the thunderbolts.

A barred slit opened and a man's eyes looked out at him. Stark dropped the hammer.

"Open up!" he shouted. "I would speak with the Lhari."

From within he heard an echo of laughter. Scraps of voices came to him on the wind, and then more laughter, and then, slowly, the great valves of the gate creaked open, wide enough only to admit him.

He stepped through, and the gateway shut behind him with a ringing clash.

He stood in a huge open court. Enclosed within its walls was a village of thatched huts, with open sheds for cooking, and behind them were pens for the stabling of beasts, the wingless dragons of the swamps that can be caught and broken to the goad.

He saw this only in vague glimpses, because of the fog. The men, who had let him in clustered around him, thrusting him forward into the light that streamed from the huts.

"He would speak with the Lhari!" one of them shouted, to the women and children who stood in the doorways watching. The words were picked up and tossed around the court, and a great burst of laughter went up.

Stark eyed them, saying nothing. They were a puzzling breed. The men, obviously, were soldiers and guards to the Lhari, for they wore the harness of fighting men. As obviously, these were their wives and children, all living behind the castle walls and having little to do with Shuruun.

But it was their racial characteristics that surprised him. They had interbred with the pale tribes of the Swamp edges that had peopled Shuruun, and there were many with milk-white hair and broad faces. Yet even these bore an alien stamp. Stark was puzzled, for the race he would have named was unknown here behind the Mountains of White Cloud, and almost unknown anywhere on Venus at Sea-level, among the sweltering marshes and the eternal fogs.

THEY stared at him even more curiously, remarking on his skin and his black hair and the unfamiliar modeling of his face. The women nudged each other and whispered, giggling, and one of them said aloud, "They'll need a barrel-hoop to collar that neck!"

The guards closed in around him. "Well, if you wish to see the Lhari, you shall," said the leader, "but first we must make sure of you."

Spear-points ringed him round. Stark made no resistance while they stripped him of all he had, except for his shorts and sandals. He had expected that, and it amused him, for there was little enough for them to take.

"All right," said the leader. "Come on."

The whole village turned out in the rain to escort Stark to the castle door. There was about them the same ominous interest that the people of Shuruun had had, with one difference. They knew what was supposed to happen to him, knew all about it, and were therefore doubly appreciative of the game.

The great doorway was square and plain, and yet neither crude nor ungraceful. The castle itself was built of the black stone, each block perfectly cut and fitted, and the door itself was sheathed in the same metal as the gate, darkened but not corroded.

The leader of the guard cried out to the warder, "Here is one who would speak with the Lhari!"

The warder laughed. "And so he shall! Their night is long, and dull."

He flung open the heavy door and cried the word down the hallway. Stark could hear it echoing hollowly within, and presently from the shadows came servants clad in silks and wearing jeweled collars, and from the guttural sound of their laughter Stark knew that they had no tongues.

Stark faltered, then. The doorway loomed hollowly before him, and it came to him suddenly that evil lay behind it and that perhaps Zareth was wiser than he when she warned him from the Lhari.

Then he thought of Helvi, and of other things, and lost his fear in anger. Lightning burned the sky. The last cry of the dying storm shook the ground under his feet. He thrust the grinning warder aside and strode into the castle, bringing a veil of the red fog with him, and did not listen to the closing of the door, which was stealthy and quiet as the footfall of approaching Death.

Torches burned here and there along the walls, and by their smoky glare he could see that the hall way was like the entrance—square and unadorned, faced with the black rock. It was high, and wide, and there was about the architecture a calm reflective dignity that had its own beauty, in some ways more impressive than the sensuous loveliness of the ruined palaces he had seen on Mars.

There were no carvings here, no paintings nor frescoes. It seemed that the builders had felt that the hall itself was enough, in its massive perfection of line and the somber gleam of polished stone. The only decoration was in the window embrasures. These were empty now, open to the sky with the red fog wreathing through them, but there were still scraps of jewel-toned panes clinging to the fretwork, to show what they had once been.

A strange feeling swept over Stark. Because of his wild upbringing, he was abnormally sensitive to the sort of impressions that most men receive either dully or not at all.

Walking down the hall, preceded by the tongueless creatures in their bright silks and blazing collars, he was struck by a subtle *difference* in the place. The castle itself was only an extension of the minds of its builders, a dream shaped into reality. Stark felt that that dark, cool, curiously timeless dream had not originated in a mind like his own, nor like that of any man he had ever seen.

Then the end of the hall was reached, the way barred by low broad doors of gold fashioned in the same chaste simplicity.

A soft scurrying of feet, a shapeless tittering from the servants, a glancing of malicious, mocking eyes. The golden doors swung open, and Stark was in the presence of the Lhari.

CHAPTER FIVE

THEY HAD THE APPEARANCE in that first glance, of

creatures glimpsed in a fever-dream, very bright and distant, robed in a misty glow that gave them an illusion of unearthly beauty.

The place in which the Earthman now stood was like a cathedral for breadth and loftiness. Most of it was in darkness, so that it seemed to reach without limit above and on all sides, as though the walls were only shadowy phantasms of the night itself. The polished black stone under his feet held a dim translucent gleam, depthless as water in a black ocean storm. There was no substance anywhere.

Far away in this shadowy vastness burned a cluster of lamps, a galaxy of little stars to shed a silvery light upon the Lords of Shuruun. There had been no sound in the place when Stark entered, for the opening of the golden doors had caught the attention of the Lhari and held it in contemplation of the stranger. Stark began to walk toward them in this utter stillness.

Quite suddenly, in the impenetrable gloom somewhere to his right, there came a sharp scuffling and a scratching of reptilian claws, a hissing and a sort of low angry muttering, all magnified and distorted by the echoing vault into a huge demoniac whispering that swept all around him.

Stark whirled around, crouched and ready, his eyes blazing and his body bathed in cold sweat. The noise increased, rushing toward him. From the distant glow of the lamps came a woman's tinkling laughter, thin crystal broken against the vault. The hissing and snarling rose to hollow crescendo, and Stark saw a blurred shape bounding at him.

His hands reached out to receive the rush, but it never came. The strange shape resolved itself into a boy of about ten, who dragged after him on a bit of rope a young two-headed dragon, new and toothless from the egg, and protesting with all its strength.

Stark straightened up, feeling let down and furious—and

relieved. The boy scowled at him through a forelock of silver curls. Then he called him a very dirty word and rushed away, kicking and hauling at the little beast until it raged like the father of all dragons and sounded like it, too, in that vast echo chamber.

A voice spoke. Slow, harsh, sexless, it rang thinly through the vault. Thin—but a steel blade is thin, too. It speaks inexorably, and its word is final.

The voice said, "Come here, into the light."

Stark obeyed the voice. As he approached the lamps, the aspect of the Lhari changed and steadied. Their beauty remained, but it was not the same. They had looked like angels. Now that he could see them clearly, Stark thought that they might have been the children of Lucifer himself.

There were six of them, counting the boy. Two men, about the same age as Stark, with some complicated gambling game forgotten between them. A woman, beautiful, gowned in white silk, sitting with her hands in her lap, doing nothing. A woman, younger, not so beautiful perhaps, but with a look of stormy and bitter vitality. She wore a short tunic of crimson, and a stout leather glove on her left hand, where perched a flying thing of prey with its fierce eyes hooded.

The boy stood beside the two men, his head poised arrogantly. From time to time he cuffed the little dragon, and it snapped at him with its impotent jaws. He was proud of himself for doing that. Stark wondered how he would behave with the beast when it had grown its fangs.

Opposite him, crouched on a heap of cushions, was a third man. He was deformed, with an ungainly body and long spidery arms, and in his lap a sharp knife lay on a block of wood, half formed into the shape of an obese creature half woman, half pure evil. Stark saw with a flash of surprise that the face of the deformed young man, of all the faces there, was truly human, truly beautiful. His eyes were old in his boyish face, wise, and very sad in their wisdom. He smiled upon the stranger, and his smile was more compassionate than tears.

THEY looked at Stark, all of them, with restless, hungry eyes. They were the pure breed, which had left its stamp of alienage on the pale-haired folk of the swamps, the serfs who dwelt in the huts outside.

They were of the Cloud People, the folk of the High Plateaus, kings of the land on the farther slopes of the Mountains of White Cloud. It was strange to see them here, on the dark side of the barrier wall, but here they were. How they had come, and why, leaving their rich cool plains for the fetor of these foreign swamps, he could not guess. But there was no mistaking them—the proud fine shaping of their bodies, their alabaster skin, their eyes that were all colors and none, like the dawn sky, their hair that was pure warm silver.

They did not speak. They seemed to be waiting for permission to speak, and Stark wondered which one of them had voiced that steely summons.

Then it came again. "Come here—come closer." And he looked beyond them, beyond the circle of lamps into the shadows again, and saw the speaker.

She lay upon a low bed, her head propped on silken pillows, her vast, her incredibly gigantic body covered with a silken pall. Only her arms were bare, two shapeless masses of white flesh ending in tiny hands. From time to time she stretched one out and took a morsel of food from the supply laid ready beside her, snuffling and wheezing with the effort, and then gulped the tidbit down with a horrible voracity.

Her features had long ago dissolved into a shaking formlessness, with the exception of her nose, which rose out of the fat, curved and cruel and thin, like the bony beak of the creature that sat on the girl's wrist and dreamed its hooded dreams of blood. And her eyes...

Stark looked into her eyes and shuddered. Then he glanced at the carving half formed in the cripple's lap, and knew what thought had guided the knife.

Half woman, half pure evil. And strong. Very strong. Her strength lay naked in her eyes for all to see, and it was an ugly strength. It could tear down mountains, but it could never build.

He saw her looking at him. Her eyes bored into his as though they would search out his very guts and study them, and he knew that she expected him to turn away, unable to bear her gaze. He did not. Presently he smiled and said, "I have outstared a rock-lizard, to determine which of us should eat the other. And I've outstared the very rock while waiting for him."

She knew that he spoke the truth. Stark expected her to be angry, but she was not. A vague mountainous rippling shook her and emerged at length as a voiceless laughter.

"You see that?" she demanded, addressing the others. "You whelps of the Lhari—not one of you dares to face me down, yet here is a great dark creature from the gods know where who can stand and shame you."

She glanced again at Stark. "What demon's blood brought you forth, that you have learned neither prudence nor fear?"

Stark answered somberly, "I learned them both before I could walk. But I learned another thing also—a thing called anger."

"And you are angry?"

"Ask Malthor if I am, and why."

He saw the two men start a little, and a slow smile crossed the girl's face.

"Malthor," said the hulk upon the bed, and ate a mouthful of roast meat dripping with fat. "That is interesting. But rage against Malthor did not bring you here. I am curious,

Stranger. Speak."

"I will."

STARK glanced around. The place was a tomb, a trap.
The very air smelled of danger. The younger folk watched
him in silence. Not one of them had spoken since he came
in, except the boy who had cursed him, and that was
unnatural in itself. The girl leaned forward, idly stroking the
creature on her wrist so that it stirred and ran its knife-like
talons in and out of their bony sheathes with sensuous
pleasure. Her gaze on Stark was bold and cool, oddly
challenging. Of them all, she alone saw him as a man. To the
others he was a problem, a diversion—something less than
human.

Stark said, "A man came to Shuruun at the time of the last
rains. His name was Helvi, and he was son of a little king by
Yarell. He came seeking his brother, who had broken tabu
and fled for his life. Helvi came to tell him that the ban was
lifted, and he might return. Neither one came back."

The small evil eyes were amused, blinking in their tallowy
creases. "And so?"

"And so I have come after Helvi, who is my friend."

Again there was the heaving of that bulk of flesh, the
explosion of laughter that hissed and wheezed in snakelike
echoes through the vault.

"Friendship must run deep with you, Stranger. Ah, well.
The Lhari are kind of heart. You shall find your friend."

And as though that were the signal to end their deferential
silence, the younger folk burst into laughter also, until the
vast hall rang with it, giving back a sound like demons
laughing on the edge of Hell.

The cripple only did not laugh, but bent his bright head
over his carving, and sighed.

The girl sprang up. "Not yet, Grandmother! Keep him

awhile."

The cold, cruel eyes shifted to her. "And what will you do with him, Varra? Haul him about on a string, like Bor with his wretched beast?"

"Perhaps—though I think it would need a stout chain to hold him." Varra turned and looked at Stark, bold and bright, taking in the breadth and the height of him, the shaping of the great smooth muscles, the iron line of the jaw. She smiled. Her mouth was very lovely, like the red fruit of the swamp tree that bears death in its pungent sweetness.

"Here is a man," she said. "The first man I have seen since my father died."

The two men at the gaming table rose, their faces flushed and angry. One of them strode forward and gripped the girl's arm roughly.

"So I am not a man," he said, with surprising gentleness. "A sad thing, for one who is to be your husband. It's best that we settle that now, before we wed."

Varra nodded. Stark saw that the man's fingers were cutting savagely into the firm muscle of her arm, but she did not wince.

"High time to settle it all, Egil. You have borne enough from me. The day is long overdue for my taming. I must learn now to bend my neck, and acknowledge my lord."

For a moment Stark thought she meant it, the note of mockery in her voice was so subtle. Then the woman in white, who all this time had not moved nor changed expression, voiced again the thin, tinkling laugh he had heard once before. From that, and the dark suffusion of blood in Egil's face, Stark knew that Varra was only casting the man's own phrases back at him. The boy let out one derisive bark, and was cuffed into silence.

Varra looked straight at Stark. "Will you fight for me?" she demanded.

Quite suddenly, it was Stark's turn to laugh. "No!" he said.

Varra shrugged. "Very well, then. I must fight for myself."

"Man," snarled Egil. "I'll show you who's a man, you scapegrace little vixen."

He wrenched off his girdle with his free hand, at the same time bending the girl around so he could get a fair shot at her. The creature of prey, a Terran falcon, clung to her wrist, beating its wings and screaming, its hooded head jerking.

WITH a motion so quick that it was hardly visible, Varra slipped the hood and flew the creature straight for Egil's face.

He let go, flinging up his arms to ward off the talons and the tearing beak. The wide wings beat and hammered. Egil yelled. The boy Bor got out of range and danced up and down shrieking with delight.

Varra stood quietly. The bruises were blackening on her arm, but she did not deign to touch them. Egil blundered against the gaming table and sent the ivory pieces flying. Then he tripped over a cushion and fell flat, and the hungry talons ripped his tunic to ribbons down the back.

Varra whistled, a clear peremptory call. The creature gave a last peck at the back of Egil's head and flopped sullenly back to its perch on her wrist. She held it, turning toward Stark. He knew from the poise of her that she was on the verge of launching her pet at him. But she studied him and then shook her head.

"No," she said, and slipped the hood back on. "You would kill it."

Egil had scrambled up and gone off into the darkness, sucking a cut on his arm. His face was black with rage. The other man looked at Varra.

"If you were pledged to me," he said, "I'd have that

temper out of you."

"Come and try it," answered Varra.

The man shrugged and sat down. "It's not my place. I keep the peace in my own house." He glanced at the woman in white, and Stark saw that her face, hitherto blank of any expression, had taken on a look of abject fear.

"You do," said Varra, "and, if I were Arel, I would stab you while you slept. But you're safe. She had no spirit to begin with."

Arel shivered and looked steadfastly at her hands. The man began to gather up the scattered pieces. He said casually, "Egil will wring your neck some day, Varra, and I shan't weep to see it."

All this time the old woman had eaten and watched, watched and eaten, her eyes glittering with interest.

"A pretty brood, are they not?" she demanded of Stark. "Full of spirit, quarrelling like young hawks in the nest. That's why I keep them around me, so—they are such sport to watch. All except Treon there." She indicated the crippled youth. "He does nothing. Dull and soft-mouthed, worse than Arel. What a grandson to be cursed with! But his sister has fire enough for two." She munched a sweet, grunting with pride.

Treon raised his head and spoke, and his voice was like music, echoing with an eerie liveliness in that park place.

"Dull I may be, Grandmother, and weak in body, and without hope. Yet I shall be the last of the Lhari. Death sits waiting on the towers, and he shall gather you all before me. I know, for the winds have told me."

He turned his suffering eyes upon Stark and smiled, a smile of such woe and resignation that the Earthman's heart ached with it. Yet there was a thankfulness in it too, as though some long waiting was over at last.

"You," he said softly, "Stranger with the fierce eyes. I saw you come, out of the darkness, and where you set foot there was a bloody print. Your arms were red to the elbows, and your breast was splashed with the redness, and on your brow was the symbol of death. Then I knew, and the wind whispered into my ear, 'It is so. This man shall pull the castle down, and its stones shall crush Shuruun and set the Lost Ones free'."

He laughed, very quietly. "Look at him, all of you. For he will be your doom."

There was a moment's silence, and Stark, with all the superstitions of a wild race thick within him, turned cold to the roots of his hair. Then the old woman said disgustedly, "Have the winds warned you of this, my idiot?"

And with astonishing force and accuracy she picked up a ripe fruit and flung it at Treon.

"Stop your mouth with that," she told him. "I am weary to death of your prophecies."

TREON looked at the crimson juice trickling slowly down the breast of his tunic, to drip upon the carving in his lap. The half-formed head was covered with it. Treon was shaken with silent mirth.

"Well," said Varra, coming up to Stark, "what do you think of the Lhari? The proud Lhari, who would not stoop to mingle their blood with the cattle of the swamps. My half-witted brother, my worthless cousins, that little monster Bor who is the last twig of the tree—do you wonder why I flew my falcon at Egil?"

She waited for an answer, her head thrown back, the silver curls framing her face like wisps of storm cloud. There was a swagger about her that at once irritated and delighted Stark. A hellcat, he thought, but a mighty fetching one, and bold as brass. Bold—and honest. Her lips were parted, midway between anger and a smile.

He caught her to him suddenly and kissed her, holding her slim strong body as though she were a doll. "He was in no hurry to set her down. When at last he did, he grinned and said, "Was that what you wanted?"

"Yes," answered Varra. "That was what I wanted." She spun about, her jaw set dangerously. "Grandmother..."

She got no farther. Stark saw that the old woman was attempting to sit upright, her face purpling with effort and the most terrible wrath he had ever seen.

"You," she gasped at the girl. She choked on her fury and her shortness of breath, and then Egil came soft-footed into the light, bearing in his hand a thing made of black metal and oddly shaped, with a blunt, thick muzzle.

"Lie back, Grandmother," he said. "I had a mind to use this on Varra—"

Even as he spoke he pressed a stud, and Stark in the act of leaping for the sheltering darkness, crashed down and lay like a dead man. There had been no sound, no flash, nothing, but a vast hand that smote him suddenly into oblivion.

Egil finished, "but I see a better target."

CHAPTER SIX

RED. RED. RED. THE COLOR of blood. Blood in his eyes. He was remembering now. The quarry had turned on him, and they had fought on the bare, blistering rocks.

Nor had N'Chaka killed. The Lord of the Rocks was very big, a giant among lizards, and N'Chaka was small. The Lord of the Rocks had laid open N'Chaka's head before the wooden spear had more than scratched his flank.

It was strange that N'Chaka still lived.

The Lord of the Rocks must have been full fed. Only that had saved him.

N'Chaka groaned, not with pain, but with shame. He had

failed. Hoping for a great triumph, he had disobeyed the tribal law that forbids a boy to hunt the quarry of a man, and he had failed. Old One would not reward him with the girdle and the flint spear of manhood. Old One would give him to the women for the punishment of little whips. Tika would laugh at him, and it would be many seasons before Old One would grant him permission to try the Man's Hunt.

Blood in his eyes.

He blinked to clear them. The instinct of survival was prodding him. He must arouse himself and creep away, before the Lord of the Rocks returned to eat him.

The redness would not go away. It swam and flowed, strangely sparkling. He blinked again, and tried to lift his head, and could not, and fear struck down upon him like the iron frost of night upon the rocks of the valley.

It was all wrong. He could see himself clearly, a naked boy, dizzy with pain, rising and clambering over the ledges and the shale to the safety of the cave. He could see that, and yet he could not move.

All wrong. Time, space, the universe, darkened and turned.

A voice spoke to him. A girl's voice. Not Tika's and the speech was strange.

Tika was dead. Memories rushed through his mind, the bitter things, the cruel things. Old One was dead, and all the others...

The voice spoke again, calling him by a name that was not his own.

Stark.

Memory shattered into a kaleidoscope of broken pictures, fragments, rushing, spinning. He was adrift among them. He was lost, and the terror of it brought a scream into his throat.

Soft hands touching his face, gentle words, swift and soothing. The redness cleared and steadied, though it did not go away, and quite suddenly he was himself again, with all his memories where they belonged.

HE WAS lying on his back, and Zareth, Malthor's daughter, was looking down at him. He knew now what the redness was. He had seen it too often before not to know. He was somewhere at the bottom of the Red Sea—that weird ocean in which a man can breathe.

And he could not move. That had not changed, nor gone away. His body was dead.

The terror he had felt before was nothing to the agony that filled him now. He lay entombed in his own flesh, staring up at Zareth, wanting an answer to a question he dared not ask.

She understood, from the look in his eyes.

"It's all right," she said, and smiled. "It will wear off. You'll be all right. It's only the weapon of the Lhari. Somehow it puts the body to sleep, but it will wake again."

Stark remembered the black object that Egil had held in his hands. A projector of some sort, then, beaming a current of high-frequency vibration that paralyzed the nerve centers. He was amazed. The Cloud People were barbarians themselves, though on a higher scale than the swamp-edge tribes, and certainly had no such scientific proficiency. He wondered where the Lhari had got hold of such a weapon.

It didn't really matter. Not just now. Relief swept over him, bringing him dangerously close to tears. The effect would wear off. At the moment, that was all he cared about.

He looked up at Zareth again. Her pale hair floated with the slow breathing of the sea, a milky cloud against the spark-shot crimson. He saw now that her face was drawn and shadowed, and there a terrible hopelessness in her eyes. She had been alive when he first saw her—frightened, not too bright, but fun of emotion and a certain dogged courage.

Now the spark was gone, crushed out.

She wore a collar around her white neck, a ring of dark metal with the ends fused together for all time.

"Where are we?" he asked.

And she answered, her voice carrying deep and hollow in the dense substance of the sea, "We are in the place of the Lost Ones."

Stark looked beyond her, as far as he could see, since he was unable to turn his head. And wonder came to him.

Black walls, black vault above him, a vast hall filled with the wash of the sea that slipped in streaks of whispering flame through the high embrasures. A hall that was twin to the vault of shadows where he had met the Lhari.

"There is a city," said Zareth dully. "You will see it soon. You will see nothing else until you die."

Stark said gently, "How do you come here, little one?"

"Because of my father. I will tell you all I know, which is little enough. Malthor has been slaver to the Lhari for a long time. There are a number of them among the captains of Shuruun, but that is a thing that is never spoken of—so I, his daughter, could only guess. I was sure of it when he sent me after you."

She laughed, a bitter sound. "Now I'm here, with the collar of the Lost Ones on my neck. But Malthor is here, too." She laughed again, ugly laughter to come from a young mouth. Then she looked at Stark, and her hand reached out timidly to touch his hair in what was almost a caress. Her eyes were wide, and soft, and full of tears.

"Why didn't you go into the swamps when I warned you?"

Stark answered stolidly, "Too late to worry about that now." Then, "You say Malthor is here, a slave?"

"Yes." Again, that look of wonder and admiration in her eyes. "I don't know what you said or did to the Lhari, but the Lord Egil came down in a black rage and cursed my father for a bungling fool because he could not hold you. My father whined and made excuses, and all would have been well— only his curiosity got the better of him and he asked the Lord Egil what had happened. You were like a wild beast, Malthor said, and he hoped you had not harmed the Lady Varra, as he could see from Egil's wounds that there had been trouble.

"The Lord Egil turned quite purple. I thought he was going to fall in a fit."

"Yes," said Stark. "That was the wrong thing to say." The ludicrous side of it struck him, and he was suddenly roaring with laughter. "Malthor should have kept his mouth shut!"

"Egil called his guard and ordered them to take Malthor. And when he realized what had happened, Malthor turned on me, trying to say that it was all my fault, that I let you escape."

Stark stopped laughing.

Her voice went on slowly, "Egil seemed quite mad with fury. I have heard that the Lhari are all mad, and I think it is so. At any rate, he ordered me taken too, for he wanted to stamp Malthor's seed into the mud forever. So we are here."

There was a long silence. Stark could think of no word of comfort, and as for hope, he had better wait until he was sure he could at least raise his head. Egil might have damaged him permanently, out of spite. He was surprised he wasn't dead.

He glanced again at the collar on Zareth's neck. Slave. Slave to the Lhari, in the city of the Lost Ones.

What the devil did they do with slaves, at the bottom of the sea?

The heavy gases conducted sound remarkably well, except for an odd property of diffusion which made it seem that a voice came from everywhere at once. Now, all at once, Stark became aware of a dull clamor of voices drifting towards him. He tried to see, and Zareth turned his head carefully so that he might.

The Lost Ones were returning from whatever work it was

they did.

OUT of the dim red murk beyond the open door they swam, into the long, long vastness of the hall that was filled with same red murk, moving slowly, their white bodies trailing wakes of sullen flame. The host of the damned drifting through a strange red-litten hell, weary and without hope.

One by one they sank onto pallets laid in rows on the black stone floor, and lay there, utterly exhausted, their pale hair lifting and floating with the slow eddies of the sea. And each one wore a collar.

One man did not lie down. He came toward Stark, a tall barbarian who drew himself with great strokes of his arms so that he was wrapped in wheeling sparks. Stark knew his face.

"Helvi," he said, and smiled in welcome.

"Brother!"

Helvi crouched down—a great handsome boy he had been the time Stark saw him, but he was a man now, with all the laughter turned to grim deep lines around his mouth and the bones of his face standing out like granite ridges.

"Brother," he said again, looking at Stark through a glitter of unashamed tears. "Fool." And he cursed Stark savagely because he had come to Shuruun to look for an idiot who had gone the same way, and was already as good as dead.

"Would you have followed me?" asked Stark.

"But I am only an ignorant child of the swamps," said Helvi. "You come from space, you know the other worlds, you can read and write—you should have better sense."

Stark grinned. "And I'm still an ignorant child of the rocks. So we're two fools together. Where is Tobal?"

Tobal was Helvi's brother, who had broken tabu and looked for refuge in Shuruun. Apparently he had found peace at last, for Helvi shook his head.

"A man cannot live too long under the sea. It is not enough merely to breathe and eat. Tobal overran his time, and I am close to the end of mine." He held up his hand and then swept it down sharply, watching the broken fires dance along his arms.

"The mind breaks before the body," said Helvi casually, as though it were a matter of no importance.

Zareth spoke. "Helvi has guarded you each period while the others slept."

"And not alone," said Helvi. "The little one stood with me."

"Guarded me!" said Stark. "Why?"

For answer, Helvi gestured toward a pallet not far away. Malthor lay there, his eyes half-open and full of malice, the fresh scar livid on his cheek.

"He feels," said Helvi, "that you should not have fought upon his ship."

Stark felt an inward chill of horror. To lie here helpless, watching Malthor come toward him with open fingers reaching for his helpless throat…

He made a passionate effort to move, and gave up, gasping. Helvi grinned.

"Now is the time I should wrestle you, Stark for I never could throw you before." He gave Stark's head a shake, very gentle for all its apparent roughness. "You'll be throwing me again. Sleep now, and don't worry."

He settled himself to watch, and presently in spite of himself Stark slept, with Zareth curled at his feet like a puppy.

There was no time down there in the heart of the Red Sea. No daylight, no dawn, no space of darkness. No winds blew, no rain nor storm broke the silence. Only the lazy currents whispered by on their way to nowhere, and the red sparks danced, and the great hall waited, remembering the past.

Stark waited, too. How long he never knew, but he was

used to waiting. He had learned his patience on the knees of the great mountains whose heads lift proudly into open space to look at the Sun, and he had absorbed their own contempt for time.

Little by little, life returned to his body. A mongrel guard came now and again to examine him, pricking Stark's flesh with his knife to test the reaction, so that Stark should not malinger.

He reckoned without Stark's control.

The Earthman bore his prodding without so much as a twitch until his limbs were completely his own again. Then he sprang up and pitched the man half the length of the hall, turning over and over, yelling with startled anger.

At the next period of labor, Stark was driven with the rest out into the City of the Lost Ones.

CHAPTER SEVEN

STARK HAD BEEN IN PLACES before that oppressed him with a sense of their strangeness or their wickedness— Sinharat, the lovely ruin of coral and gold lost in the Martian wastes; Jekkara, Valkis—the Low-Canal towns that smell of blood and wine; the cliff-caves of Arianrhed on the edge of Darkside, the buried tomb-cities of Callisto. But this—this was nightmare to haunt a man's dreams.

He stared about him as he went in the long line of slaves, and felt such a cold shuddering contraction of his belly as he had never known before.

Wide avenues paved with polished blocks of stone, perfect as ebon mirrors. Buildings, tall and stately, pure and plain, with a calm strength that could outlast the ages. Black, all black, with no fripperies of paint or carving to soften them, only here and there a window like a drowned jewel glinting through the red.

Vines like drifts of snow cascading down the stones. Gardens with close-clipped turf and flowers lifting bright on their green stalks, their petals open to a daylight that was gone, their head bending as though to some forgotten breeze. All neat, all tended, the branches pruned, the fresh soil turned this morning—by whose hand?

Stark remembered the great forest dreaming at the bottom of the gulf, and shivered. He did not like to think how long ago these flowers must have opened their young bloom to the last light they were ever going to see. For they were dead— dead as the forest, dead as the city. Forever bright—and dead.

Stark thought that it must always have been a silent city. It was impossible to imagine noisy throngs flocking to a market square down those immense avenues. The black walls were not made to echo song or laughter. Even the children must have moved quietly along the garden paths, small wise creatures born to an ancient dignity.

He was beginning to understand now the meaning of that weird forest. The Gulf of Shuruun had not always been a gulf. It had been a valley, rich, fertile, with this great city in its arms, and here and there on the upper slopes the retreat of some noble or philosopher—of which the castle of the Lhari was a survivor.

A wall or rock had held back the Red Sea from this valley. And then, somehow, the wall had cracked, and the sullen crimson tide had flowed slowly, slowly into the fertile bottoms, rising higher, lapping the towers and the tree-tops in swirling flame, drowning the land forever. Stark wondered if the people had known the disaster was coming, if they had gone forth to tend their gardens for the last time so that they might remain perfect in the embalming gases of the sea.

THE columns of slaves, herded by overseers armed with small black weapons similar to the one Egil had used, came out into a broad square whose farther edges were veiled in the red murk. And Stark looked on ruin.

A great building had fallen in the center of the square. The gods only knew what force had burst its walls and tossed the giant blocks like pebbles into a heap. But there it was, the one untidy thing in the city, a mountain of debris.

Nothing else was damaged. It seemed that this had been the place of temples, and they stood unharmed, ranked around the sides of the square, the dim fires rippling through their open porticoes. Deep in their inner shadows Stark thought he could make out images, gigantic things brooding in the spark-shot gloom.

He had no chance to study them. The overseers cursed them on, and now he saw what use the slaves were put to. They were clearing away the wreckage of the fallen building.

Helvi whispered, "For sixteen years men have slaved and died down here, and the work is not half done. And why do the Lhari want it done at all? I'll tell you why. Because they are mad, mad as swamp-dragons gone *musth* in the spring."

It seemed madness indeed, to labor at this pile of rocks in a dead city at the bottom of the sea. It was madness. And yet the Lhari, though they might be insane, were not fools. There was a reason for it, and Stark was sure it was a good reason—good for the Lhari, at any rate.

An overseer came up to Stark, thrusting him roughly toward a sledge already partly loaded with broken rocks. Stark hesitated, his eyes turning ugly, and Helvi said,

"Come on, you fool! Do you want to be down flat on your back again?"

Stark glanced at the little weapon, blunt and ready, and turned reluctantly to obey. And there began his servitude.

It was a weird sort of life he led. For a while he tried to reckon time by the periods of work and sleep, but he lost count, and it did not greatly matter anyway.

He labored with the others, hauling the huge blocks away, clearing out the cellars that were partly bared, shoring up weak walls underground. The slaves clung to their old habit of thought, calling the work-periods "days" and the sleep-periods "nights".

Each "day" Egil, or his brother Cond, came to see what had been done, and went away black-browed and disappointed, ordering the work speeded up.

Treon was there also much of the time. He would come slowly in his awkward crabwise way and perch like a pale gargoyle on the stones, never speaking, watching with his sad beautiful eyes. He woke a vague foreboding in Stark. There was something awesome in Treon's silent patience, as though he waited the coming of some black doom, long delayed but inevitable. Stark would remember the prophecy, and shiver.

It was, obvious to Stark after a while that the Lhari were clearing the building to get at the cellars underneath. The great dark caverns already bared had yielded nothing, but the brothers still hoped. Over and over Cond and Egil sounded the walls and the floors, prying here and there, and chafing at the delay in opening up the underground labyrinth. What they hoped to find, no one knew.

Varra came, too. Alone, and often, she would drift down through the dim mist-fires and watch, smiling a secret smile, her hair like blown silver where the currents played with it. She had nothing but curt words for Egil, but she kept her eyes on the great dark Earthman, and there was a look in them that stirred his blood. Egil was not blind, and it stirred his too, but in a different way.

ZARETH saw that look. She kept as close to Stark as possible, asking no favors, but following him around with a sort of quiet devotion, seeming contented only when she was near him. One "night" in the slave barracks she crouched beside his pallet, her hand on his bare knee. She did not speak, and her face was hidden by the floating masses of her hair.

Stark turned her head so that he could see her, pushing the pale cloud gently away.

"What troubles you, little sister?"

Her eyes were wide and shadowed with some vague fear. But she only said, "It's not my place to speak."

"Why not?"

"Because…" Her mouth trembled, and then suddenly she said, "Oh, it's foolish, I know. But the woman of the Lhari…"

"What about her?"

"She watches you. Always she watches you. And the Lord Egil is angry. There is something in her mind, and it will bring you only evil. I know it."

"It seems to me," said Stark wryly, "that the Lhari have already done as much evil as possible to all of us."

"No," answered Zareth, with an odd wisdom. "Our hearts are still clean."

Stark smiled. He leaned over and kissed her. "I'll be careful, little sister."

Quite suddenly she flung her arms around his neck and clung to him tightly, and Stark's face sobered. He patted her, rather awkwardly, and then she had gone, to curl up on her own pallet with her head buried in her arms.

Stark lay down. His heart was sad, and there was a stinging moisture in his eyes.

The red eternities dragged on. Stark learned what Helvi had meant when he said that the mind broke before the body. The sea bottom was no place for creatures of the upper air. He learned also the meaning of the metal collars, and the manner of Tobal's death.

Helvi explained.

"There are boundaries laid down. Within them we may range, if we have the strength and the desire after work. Beyond them we may not go. And there is no chance of escape by breaking through the barrier. How this is done I do not understand, but it is so, and the collars are the key to it.

"When a slave approaches the barrier the collar brightens as though with fire, and the slave falls. I have tried this myself, and I know. Half paralyzed, you may still crawl back to safety. But if you are mad, as Tobal was, and charge the barrier strongly..."

He made a cutting motion with his hands.

Stark nodded. He did not attempt to explain electricity or electronic vibrations to Helvi, but it seemed plain enough that the force with which the Lhari kept their slaves in check was something of the sort. The collars acted as conductors, perhaps for the same type of beam that was generated in the hand-weapons. When the metal broke the invisible boundary line it triggered off a force-beam from the central power station, in the manner of the obedient electric eye that opens doors and rings alarm bells. First a warning—then death.

THE boundaries were wide enough, extending around the city and enclosing a good bit of forest beyond it. There was no possibility of a slave hiding among the trees, because the collar could be traced by the same type of beam, turned to low power, and the punishment meted out to a retaken man was such that few were foolish enough to try that game.

The surface, of course, was utterly forbidden. The one unguarded spot was the island where the central power station was, and here the slaves were allowed to come sometimes at night. The Lhari had discovered that they lived longer and worked better if they had an occasional breath of air and a look at the sky.

Many times Stark made that pilgrimage with the others.

Up from the red depths they would come, through the reeling bands of fire where the currents ran, through the clouds of crimson sparks and the sullen patches of stillness that were like pools of blood, a company of white ghosts shrouded in flame, rising from their tomb for a little taste of the world they had lost.

It didn't matter that they were so weary they had barely the strength to get back to the barracks and sleep. They found the strength. To walk again on the open ground, to be rid of the eternal crimson dusk and the oppressive weight on the chest—to look up into the hot blue night of Venus and smell the fragrance of the *liha*-trees borne on the land wind…they found the strength.

They sang here, sitting on the island rocks and staring through the mists toward the shore they would never see again. It was their chanting that Stark had heard when he came down the gulf with Malthor, that wordless cry of grief and loss. Now he was here himself, holding Zareth close to comfort her and joining his own deep voice into that primitive reproach to the gods.

While he sat, howling like the savage he was, he studied the power plant, a squat blockhouse of a place. On the nights the slaves came, guards were stationed outside to warn them away. The blockhouse was doubly guarded with the shock-beam. To attempt to take it by force would only mean death for all concerned.

Stark gave that idea up for the time being. There was never a second when escape was not in his thoughts, but he was too old in the game to break his neck against a stone wall. Like Malthor, he would wait.

Zareth and Helvi both changed after Stark's coming. Though they never talked of breaking free, both of them lost their air of hopelessness. Stark made neither plans nor promises. But Helvi knew him from of old, and the girl had her own subtle understanding, and they held up their heads again.

Then, one "day" as the work was ending, Varra came smiling out of the red murk and beckoned to him, and Stark's heart gave a great leap. Without a backward look he left Helvi and Zareth, and went with her, down the wide still avenue that led outward to the forest.

CHAPTER EIGHT

THEY LEFT THE STATELY buildings and the wide spaces behind them, and went in among the trees. Stark hated the forest. The city was bad enough, but it was dead, honestly dead, except for those neat nightmare gardens. There was something terrifying about these great trees, full-leafed and green, rioting with flowering vines and all the rich undergrowth of the jungle, standing like massed corpses made lovely by mortuary art. They swayed and rustled as the coiling fires swept them, branches bending to that silent horrible parody of wind. Stark always felt trapped there, and stifled by the stiff leaves and the vines.

But he went, and Varra slipped like a silver bird between the great trunks, apparently happy.

"I have come here often, ever since I was old enough. It's wonderful. Here I can stoop and fly like one of my own hawks." She laughed and plucked a golden flower to set in her hair, and then darted away again, her white legs flashing.

Stark followed. He could see what she meant. Here in this strange sea one's motion was as much flying as swimming, since the pressure equalized the weight of the body. There was a queer sort of thrill in plunging headlong from the treetops, to arrow down through a tangle of vines and branches and then sweep upward again.

She was playing with him, and he knew it. The challenge

got his blood up. He could have caught her easily but he did not, only now and again he circled her to show his strength. They sped on and on, trailing wakes of flame, a black hawk chasing a silver dove through the forests of a dream.

But the dove had been fledged in an eagle's nest. Stark wearied of the game at last. He caught her and they clung together, drifting still among the trees with the momentum of that wonderful weightless flight.

Her kiss at first was lazy, teasing and curious. Then it changed. All Stark's smoldering anger leaped into a different kind of flame. His handling of her was rough and cruel, and she laughed, a little fierce voiceless laugh, and gave it back to him, and remembered how he had thought her mouth was like a bitter fruit that would give a man pain when he kissed it.

She broke away at last and came to rest on a broad branch, leaning back against the trunk and laughing, her eyes brilliant and cruel as Stark's own. And Stark sat down at her feet.

"What do you want?' he demanded. "What do you want with me?"

She smiled. There was nothing sidelong or shy about her. She was bold as a new blade.

"I'll tell you, wild man."

He started. "Where did you pick up that name?"

"I have been asking the Earthman Larrabee about you. It suits you well." She leaned forward. "This is what I want of you. Slay me Egil and his brother Cond. Also Bor, who will grow up worse than either—although that I can do myself, if you're adverse to killing children, though Bor is more monster than child. Grandmother can't live forever, and with my cousins out of the way she's no threat. Treon doesn't count."

"And if I do—what then?"

"Freedom. And me. You'll rule Shuruun at my side."

Stark's eyes were mocking. "For how long, Varra?"

"Who knows? And what does it matter? The years take care of themselves." She shrugged. "The Lhari blood has run out, and it's time there was a fresh strain. Our children will rule after us, and they'll be men."

Stark laughed. He roared with it.

"It's not enough that I'm a slave to the Lhari. Now I must be executioner and herd bull as well." He looked at her keenly. "Why me, Varra? Why pick on me?"

"Because, as I have said, you are the first man I have seen since my father died. Also, there is something about you…"

She pushed herself upward to hover lazily, her lips just brushing his.

"Do you think it would be so bad a thing to live with me, wild man?"

She was lovely and maddening, a silver witch shining among the dim fires of the sea, full of wickedness and laughter. Stark reached out and drew her to him.

"Not bad," he murmured. "Dangerous."

He kissed her, and she whispered, "I think you're not afraid of danger."

"On the contrary, I'm a cautious man." He held her off, where he could look straight into her eyes. "I owe Egil something on my own, but I will not murder. The fight must be fair, and Cond will have to take care of himself."

"Fair! Was Egil fair with you—or me?"

He shrugged. "My way, or not at all."

SHE thought it over a while, then nodded. "All right. As for Cond, you will give him a blood debt, and pride will make him fight. The Lhari are all proud," she added bitterly. "That's our curse. But it's bred in the bone, as you'll find out."

"One more thing. Zareth and Helvi are to go free, and

there must be an end to this slavery."

She stared at him. "You drive a hard bargain, wild man."

"Yes or no?"

Yes *and* no. Zareth and Helvi you may have, if you insist, though the gods know what you see in that pallid child. As to the other..." She smiled very mockingly. "I'm no fool, Stark. You're evading me, and two can play that game."

He laughed. "Fair enough. And now tell me this, witch with the silver curls—how am I to get at Egil that I may kill him?"

"I'll arrange that."

She said it with such vicious assurance that he was pretty sure she would arrange it. He was silent for a moment, and then he asked,

"Varra—what are the Lhari searching for at the bottom of the sea?"

She answered slowly, "I told you that we are a proud clan. We were driven out of the High Plateaus centuries ago because of our pride. Now it's all we have left, but it's a driving thing."

She paused, and then went on. "I think we had known about the city for a long time, but it had never meant anything until my father became fascinated by it. He would stay down here days at a time, exploring, and it was he who found the weapons and the machine of power that is on the island. Then he found the chart and the metal book, hidden away in a secret place. The book was written in pictographs—as though it was meant to be deciphered—and the chart showed the square with the ruined building and the temples, with a separate diagram of catacombs underneath the ground.

"The book told of a secret—a thing of wonder and of fear. And my father believed that the building had been wrecked to close the entrance to the catacombs where the secret was kept. He determined to find it."

Sixteen years of other men's lives. Stark shivered. "What was the secret, Varra?"

"The manner of controlling life. How it was done I do not know, but with it one might build a race of giants, of monsters, or of gods. You can see what that would mean to us, a proud and dying clan."

"Yes," Stark answered slowly. "I can see."

The magnitude of the idea shook him. The builders of the city must have been wise indeed in their scientific research to evolve such a terrible power. To mold the living cells of the body to one's will—to create, not life itself but its form and fashion...

A race of giants, or of gods. The Lhari would like that. To transform their own degenerate flesh into something beyond the race of men, to develop their followers into a corps of fighting men that no one could stand against, to see that their children were given an unholy advantage over all the children of men...Stark was appalled at the realization of the evil they could do if they ever found that secret.

Varra said, "There was a warning in the book. The meaning of it was not quite clear, but it seemed that the ancient ones felt that they had sinned against the gods and been punished, perhaps by some plague. They were a strange race, and not human. At any rate, they destroyed the great building there as a barrier against anyone who should come after them, and then let the Red Sea in to cover their city forever. They must have been superstitious children, for all their knowledge."

"Then you all ignored the warning, and never worried that a whole city had died to prove it."

She shrugged. "Oh, Treon has been muttering prophecies about it for years. Nobody listens to him. As for myself, I don't care whether we find the secret or not. My belief is it was destroyed along with the building, and besides, I have no faith in such things."

"Besides," mocked Stark shrewdly, "you wouldn't care to see Egil and Cond striding across the heavens of Venus, and you're doubtful just what your own place would be in the new pantheon."

She showed her teeth at him. "You're too wise for your own good. And now good-bye." She gave him a quick, hard kiss and was gone, flashing upward, high above the treetops where he dared not follow.

Stark made his way slowly back to the city, upset and very thoughtful.

As he came back into the great square, heading toward the barracks, he stopped, every nerve taut.

Somewhere, in one of the shadowy temples, the clapper of a votive bell was swinging, sending its deep pulsing note across the silence. Slowly, slowly, like the beating of a dying heart it came, and mingled with it was the faint sauna of Zareth's voice, calling his name.

CHAPTER NINE

HE CROSSED THE SQUARE, moving very carefully through the red murk, and presently he saw her.

It was not hard to find her. There was one temple larger than all the rest. Stark judged that it must once have faced the entrance of the fallen building, as though the great figure within was set to watch over the scientists and the philosophers who came there to dream their vast and sometimes terrible dreams.

The philosophers were gone, and the scientists had destroyed themselves. But the image still watched over the drowned city, its hand raised both in warning and in benediction.

Now, across its reptilian knees, Zareth lay. The temple

was open on all sides, and Stark could see her clearly, a little white scrap of humanity against the black unhuman figure.

Malthor stood beside her. It was he who had been tolling the votive bell. He had stopped now, and Zareth's words came clearly to Stark.

"Go away, go away! They're waiting for you. Don't come in here."

"I'm waiting for you, Stark," Malthor called out, smiling. "Are you afraid to come?" And he took Zareth by the hair and struck her, slowly and deliberately, twice across the face.

All expression left Stark's face, leaving it perfectly blank except for his eyes, which took on a sudden lambent gleam. He began to move toward the temple, not hurrying even then, but moving in such a way that it seemed an army could not have stopped him.

Zareth broke free from her father. Perhaps she was intended to break free.

"Egil!" she screamed. "It's a trap…"

Again Malthor caught her and this time he struck her harder, so that she crumpled down again across the image that watched with its jeweled, gentle eyes and saw nothing.

"She's afraid for you," said Malthor. "She knows I mean to kill you if I can. Well, perhaps Egil is here also. Perhaps he is not. But certainly Zareth is here. I have beaten her well, and I shall beat her again, as long as she lives to be beaten, for her treachery to me. And if you want to save her from that, you outland dog, you'll have to kill me. Are you afraid?"

Stark was afraid. Malthor and Zareth were alone in the temple. The pillared colonnades were empty except for the dim fires of the sea. Yet Stark was afraid, for an instinct older than speech warned him to be.

It did not matter. Zareth's white skin was mottled with dark bruises, and Malthor was smiling at him, and it did not matter.

Under the shadow of the roof and down the colonnade he went, swiftly now, leaving a streak of fire behind him. Malthor looked into his eyes, and his smile trembled and was gone.

He crouched. And at the last moment, when the dark body plunged down at him as a shark plunges, he drew a hidden knife from his girdle and struck.

Stark had not counted on that. The slaves were searched for possible weapons every day, and even a sliver of stone was forbidden. Somebody must have given it to him, someone...

The thought flashed through his mind while he was in the very act of trying to avoid that deathblow. *Too late, too late, because his own momentum carried him onto the point....*

Reflexes quicker than any man's, the hair-trigger reactions of a wild thing. Muscles straining, the center of balance shifted with an awful wrenching effort, hands grasping at the fire-shot redness as though to force it to defy its own laws. The blade ripped a long shallow gash across his breast. But it did not go home. By a fraction of an inch, it did not go home.

While Stark was still off balance, Malthor sprang.

THEY grappled. The knife blade glittered redly, a hungry tongue eager to taste Stark's life. The two men rolled over and over, drifting and tumbling erratically, churning the sea to a froth of sparks, and still the image watched, it's calm reptilian features unchangingly benign and wise. Threads of a darker red laced heavily across the dancing fires.

Stark got Malthor's arm under his own and held it there with both hands. His back was to the man now. Malthor kicked and clawed with his feet against the backs of Stark's thighs, and his left arm came up and tried to clamp around Stark's throat. Stark buried his chin so that it could not, and then Malthor's hand began to tear at Stark's face, searching for his eyes.

Stark voiced a deep bestial sound in his throat. He moved his head suddenly, catching Malthor's hand between his jaws. He did not let go. Presently his teeth were locked against the thumb-joint, and Malthor was screaming, but Stark could give all his attention to what he was doing with the arm that held the knife. His eyes had changed. They were all beast now, the eyes of a killer blazing cold and beautiful in his dark face.

There was a dull crack, and the arm ceased to strain or fight. It bent back upon itself, and the knife fell, drifting quietly down. Malthor was beyond screaming now. He made one effort to get away as Stark released him, but it was a futile gesture, and he made no sound as Stark broke his neck.

He thrust the body from him. It drifted away, moving lazily with the suck of the currents through the colonnade, now and again touching a black pillar as though in casual wonder, wandering out at last into the square. Malthor was in no hurry. He had all eternity before him.

Stark moved carefully away from the girl, who was trying feebly now to set up on the knees of the image. He called out, to some unseen presence hidden in the shadows under the roof.

"Malthor screamed your name, Egil. Why didn't you come?"

There was a flicker of movement in the intense darkness of the ledge at the top of the pillars.

"Why should I?" asked the Lord Egil of the Lhari. "I offered him his freedom if he could kill you, but it seems he could not—even though I gave him a knife, and drugs to keep your friend Helvi out of the way."

He came out where Stark could see him, very handsome in a tunic of yellow silk, the blunt black weapon in his hands.

"The important thing was to bait a trap. You would not face me because of this—" He raised the weapon. "I might have killed you as you worked, of course, but my family would have had hard things to say about that. You're a phenomenally good slave."

"They'd have said hard words like 'coward', Egil," Stark said softly. "And Varra would have set her bird at you in earnest."

Stark voiced a deep bestial sound in his throat.

Egil nodded. His lip curved cruelly.

"Exactly. That amused you, didn't it? And now my little cousin is training another falcon to swoop at me. She hooded you today, didn't she, Outlander?"

190

He laughed. "Ah well. I didn't kill you openly because there's a better way. Do you think I want it gossiped all over the Red Sea that my cousin jilted me for a foreign slave? Do you think I wish it known that I hated you, and why? No. I would have killed Malthor anyway, if you hadn't done it, because he knew. And when I have killed you and the girl I shall take your bodies to the barrier and leave them there together, and it will be obvious to everyone, even Varra, that you were killed trying to escape."

The weapon's muzzle pointed straight at Stark, and Egil's finger quivered on the trigger stud. Full power, this time. Instead of paralysis, death. Stark measured the distance between himself and Egil. He would be dead before he struck, but the impetus of his leap might carry him on, and give Zareth a chance to escape. The muscles of his thighs stirred and tensed.

A voice said, "And it will be obvious how and why I died, Egil? For if you kill them, you must kill me too."

WHERE Treon had come from, or when, Stark did not know. But he was there by the image, and his voice was full of a strong music, and his eyes shone with a fey light.

Egil had started, and now he swore in fury. "You idiot! You twisted freak! How did you come here?"

"How does the wind come, and the rain? I am not as other men." He laughed, a somber sound with no mirth in it. "I am here, Egil, and that's all that matters. And you will not slay this stranger who is more beast than man, and more man than any of us. The gods have a use for him."

He had moved as he spoke, until now he stood between Stark and Egil.

"Get out of the way," said Egil.

Treon shook his head.

"Very well," said Egil. "If you wish to die, you may."

The fey gleam brightened in Treon's eyes. "This is a day of death," he said softly, "but not of his, or mine."

Egil said a short, ugly word, and raised the weapon up.

Things happened very quickly after that. Stark sprang, arching up and over Treon's head, cleaving the red gasses like a burning arrow. Egil started back, and shifted his aim upward, and his finger snapped down on the trigger stud.

Something white came between Stark and Egil, and took the force of the bolt.

Something white. A girl's body, crowned with streaming hair, and a collar of metal glowing bright around the slender neck.

Zareth.

They had forgotten her, the beaten child crouched on the knees of the image. Stark had moved to keep her out of danger, and she was no threat to the mighty Egil, and Treon's thoughts were known only to himself and the winds that taught him. Unnoticed, she had crept to a place where one last plunge would place her between Stark and death.

The rush of Stark's going took him on over her, except that her hair brushed softly against his skin. Then he was on top of Egil, and it had all been done so swiftly that the Lord of the Lhari had not had time to loose another bolt.

Stark tore the weapon from Egil's hand. He was cold, icy cold, and there was a strange blindness on him, so that he could see nothing clearly but Egil's face. And it was Stark who screamed this time, a dreadful sound like the cry of a great cat gone beyond reason or fear.

Treon stood watching. He watched the blood stream darkly into the sea, and he listened to the silence come, and he saw the thing that had been his cousin drift away on the slow tide, and it was as though he had seen it all before and was not surprised.

Stark went to Zareth's body. The girl was still breathing,

very faintly, and her eyes turned to Stark, and she smiled.

Stark was blind now with tears. All his rage had run out of him with Egil's blood, leaving nothing but an aching pity and a sadness, and a wondering awe. He took Zareth very tenderly into his arms and held her, dumbly, watching the tears fall on her upturned face. And presently he knew that she was dead.

Sometime later Treon came to him and said softly, "To this end she was born, and she knew it, and was happy. Even now she smiles. And she should, for she had a better death than most of us." He laid his hand on Stark's shoulder. "Come, I'll show you where to put her. She will be safe there, and tomorrow you can bury her where she would wish to be."

Stark rose and followed him, bearing Zareth in his arms.

Treon went to the pedestal on which the image sat. He pressed in a certain way upon a series of hidden springs, and a section of the paving slid noiselessly back, revealing stone steps leading down.

CHAPTER TEN

TREON LED THE WAY DOWN, into darkness that was lightened only by the dim fires they themselves woke in passing. No currents ran here. The red gas lay dull and stagnant, closed within the walls of a square passage built of the same black stone.

"These are the crypts," he said. "The labyrinth that is shown on the chart my father found." And he told about the chart, as Varra had.

He led the way surely, his misshapen body moving without hesitation past the mouths of branching corridors and the doors of chambers whose interiors were lost in shadow.

"The history of the city is here. All the books and the learning, that they had not the heart to destroy. There are no weapons. They were not a warlike people, and I think that the force we of the Lhari have used differently was defensive only, protection against the beasts and the raiding primitives of the swamps."

With a great effort, Stark wrenched his thoughts away from the light burden he carried.

"I thought," he said dully, "that the crypts were under the wrecked building."

"So we all thought. We were intended to think so. That is why the building was wrecked. And for sixteen years we of the Lhari have killed men and women with dragging the stones of it away. But the temple was shown also in the chart. We thought it was there merely as a landmark, an identification for the great building. But I began to wonder…"

"How long have you known?"

"Not long. Perhaps two rains. It took many seasons to find the secret of this passage. I came here at night, when the others slept."

"And you didn't tell?"

"No," said Treon. "You are thinking that if I had told, there would have been an end to the slavery and the death. But what then? My family, turned loose with the power to destroy a world, as this city was destroyed? No. It was better for the slaves to die."

He motioned Stark aside, then, between doors of gold that stood ajar, into a vault so great that there was no guessing its size in the red and shrouding gloom.

"This was the burial place of their kings," said Treon softly. "Leave the little one here."

Stark looked around him, still too numb to feel awe, but impressed even so.

They were set in straight lines, the beds of black marble— lines so long that there was no end to them except the limit of vision. And on them slept the old kings, their bodies, marvelously embalmed, covered with silken palls, their hands crossed upon their breasts, their wise unhuman faces stamped with the mark of peace.

Very gently, Stark laid Zareth down on a marble couch, and covered her also with silk, and closed her eyes and folded her hands. And it seemed to him that her face, too, had that look of peace.

He went out with Treon, thinking that none of them had earned a better place in the hall of kings than Zareth.

"Treon," he said.

"Yes?"

"That prophecy you spoke when I came to the castle—I will bear it out."

Treon nodded. "That is the way of prophecies."

He did not return toward the temple, but led the way deeper into the heart of the catacombs. A great excitement burned within him, a bright and terrible thing that communicated itself to Stark. Treon had suddenly taken on the stature of a figure of destiny, and the Earthman had the feeling that he was in the grip of some current that would plunge on irresistibly until everything in its path was swept away. Stark's flesh quivered.

THEY reached the corridor's end at last. There, in the red gloom, a shape sat waiting before a black, barred door. A shape grotesque and incredibly misshapen, so horribly malformed that by it Treon's crippled body appeared almost beautiful. Yet its face was as the faces of the images and the old kings, and its sunken eyes had once held wisdom, and one of its seven-fingered hands were still slim and sensitive.

Stark recoiled. The thing made him physically sick, and he would have turned away, but Treon urged him on.

"Go closer. It is dead, embalmed, but it has a message for

you. It has waited all this time to give that message."

Reluctantly, Stark went forward.

Quite suddenly, it seemed that the thing spoke.

Behold me. Look upon me, and take counsel before you grasp that power which lies beyond the door!

Stark leaped back, crying out, and Treon smiled.

"It was so with me. But I have listened to it many times since then. It speaks not with a voice, but within the mind, and only when one has passed a certain spot."

Stark's reasoning mind pondered over that. A thought-record, obviously, triggered off by an electronic beam. The ancients had taken good care that their warning would be heard and understood by anyone who should solve the riddle of the catacombs. Thought-images, speaking directly to the brain, know no barrier of time or language.

He stepped forward again, and once more the telepathic voice spoke to him.

"We tampered with the secrets of the gods. We intended no evil. It was only that we love perfection, and wished to shape all living things as flawless as our buildings and our gardens. We did not know that it was against the Law...

"I was one of those who found the way to change the living cell. We used the unseen force that comes from the Land of the Gods beyond the sky, and we so harnessed it that we could build from the living flesh as the potter builds from the clay. We healed the halt and the maimed, and made those stand tall and straight who came crooked from the egg, and for a time we were as brothers to the gods themselves. I myself, even I, knew the glory of perfection. And then came the reckoning.

'The cell, once made to change, would not stop changing. The growth was slow, and for a while we did not notice it, but when we did it was too late. We were becoming a city of monsters. And the force we had used was worse than useless, for the more we tried to mould the monstrous flesh to its normal shape, the more the stimulated cells grew and grew, until the bodies we labored over were like things of wet mud that flow and change even as you look at them.

"One by one the people of the city destroyed themselves. And those of us who were left realized the judgment of the gods, and our duty. We made all things ready, and let the Red Sea hide us forever from our own kind, and those who should come after.

"Yet we did not destroy our knowledge. Perhaps it was our pride only that forbade us, but we could not bring ourselves to do it. Perhaps other gods, other races wiser than we, can take away the evil and keep only the good. For it is good for all creatures to be, if not perfect, at least strong and sound.

"But heed this warning, whoever you may be that listen. If your gods are jealous, if your people have not the wisdom or the knowledge to succeed where we failed in controlling this force, then touch it not! Or you, and all your people, will become as I."

THE voice stopped. Stark moved back again, and said to Treon incredulously, "And your family would ignore that warning?"

Treon laughed. "They are fools. They are cruel and greedy and very proud. They would say that this was a lie to frighten away intruders, or that human flesh would not be subject to the laws that govern the flesh of reptiles. They would say anything, because they have dreamed this dream too long to be denied."

Stark shuddered and looked at the black door. "The thing ought to be destroyed."

"Yes," said Treon softly.

His eyes were shining, looking into some private dream of

his own. He started forward, and when Stark would have gone with him he thrust him back, saying, "No. You have no part in this." He shook his head.

"I have waited," he whispered, almost to himself. "The winds bade me wait until the day was ripe to fall from the tree of death. I have waited, and at dawn I knew, for the wind said, *Now is the gathering of the fruit at hand.*"

He looked suddenly at Stark, and his eyes had in them a clear sanity, for all their feyness.

"You heard, Stark. 'We made those stand tall and straight who came crooked from the egg. I will have my hour. I will stand as a man for the little time that is left."

He turned, and Stark made no move to follow. He watched Treon's twisted body recede, white against the red dusk, until it passed the monstrous watcher and came to the black door. The long thin arms reached up and pushed the bar away.

The door swung slowly back. Through the opening Stark glimpsed a chamber that held a structure of crystal rods and discs mounted on a frame of metal, the whole thing glowing and glittering with a restless bluish light that dimmed and brightened as though it echoed some vast pulse-beat. There was other apparatus, intricate banks of tubes and condensers, but this was the heart of it; and the heart was still alive.

Treon passed within and closed the door behind him.

Stark drew back some distance from the door and its guardian, crouched down, and set his back against the wall. He thought about the apparatus. Cosmic rays, perhaps—the unseen force that came from beyond the sky. Even yet, all their potentialities were not known. But a few luckless spacemen had found that under certain conditions they could do amazing things to human tissue.

It was a line of thought Stark did not like at all. He tried to keep his mind away from Treon entirely. He tried not to think at all. It was dark there in the corridor, and very still, and the shapeless horror sat quiet in the doorway and waited with him. Stark began to shiver—a shallow animal-twitching of the flesh.

He waited. After a while he thought Treon must be dead, but he did not move. He did not wish to go into that room to see.

He waited.

Suddenly he leaped up, cold sweat all over him. A crash had echoed down the corridor, a clashing of shattered crystal and a high singing note that trailed off into nothing.

The door opened.

A man came out. A man tall and straight and beautiful as an angel, a strong-limbed man with Treon's face, Treon's tragic eyes. And behind him the chamber was dark. The pulsing heart of power had stopped.

The door was shut and barred again. Treon's voice was saying, "There are records left, and much of the apparatus, so that the secret is not lost entirely. Only it is out of reach."

He came to Stark and held out his hand. "Let us fight together, as men. And do not fear. I shall die, long before this body changes." He smiled, the remembered smile that was full of pity for all living things. "I know, for the winds have told me."

Stark took his hand and held it.

"Good," said Treon. "And now lead on, stranger with the fierce eyes. For the prophecy is yours, and the day is yours, and I who have crept about like a snail all my life know little of battles. Lead, and I will follow."

Stark fingered the collar around his neck. "Can you rid me of this?"

Treon nodded. "There are tools and acid in one of the chambers."

He found them, worked swiftly. While he worked Stark

thought, smiling—and there was no pity in that smile at all.

They came back at last into the temple, and Treon closed the entrance to the catacombs. It was still night, for the square was empty of slaves. Stark found Egil's weapon where it had fallen, on the ledge where Egil died.

"We must hurry," said Stark. "Come on."

CHAPTER ELEVEN

THE ISLAND WAS SHROUDED heavily in mist and the blue darkness of the night. Stark and Treon crept silently among the rocks until they could see the glimmer of torchlight through the window-slits of the power station. There were seven guards, five inside the blockhouse, two outside to patrol.

When they were close enough, Stark slipped away, going like a shadow, and never a pebble turned under his bare foot. Presently he found a spot to his liking and crouched down. A sentry went by not three feet away, yawning and looking hopefully at the sky for the first signs of dawn.

Treon's voice rang out, the sweet unmistakable voice. "Ho, there, guards!"

The sentry stopped and whirled around. Off around the curve of the stone wall someone began to run, his sandals thud-thudding on the soft ground, and the second guard came up.

"Who speaks?" one demanded. "The Lord Treon?"

They peered into the darkness, and Treon answered, "Yes." He had come forward far enough so that they could make out the pale blur of his face, keeping his body out of sight among the rocks and the shrubs that sprang up between them.

"Make haste," he ordered. "Bid them open the door, there." He spoke in breathless jerks, as though spent. "A tragedy—a disaster! Bid them open!"

One of the men leaped to obey, hammering on the massive door that was kept barred from the inside. The other stood goggle-eyed, watching. Then the door opened, spilling a flood of yellow torchlight into the red fog.

"What is it?" cried the men inside. "What has happened?"

"Come out!" gasped Treon. "My cousin is dead, the Lord Egil is dead, murdered by a slave."

He let that sink in. Three or more men came outside into the circle of light, and their faces were frightened, as though somehow they feared they might be held responsible for this thing.

"You know him," said Treon. "The great black-haired one from Earth. He has slain the Lord Egil and got away into the forest, and we need all extra guards to go after him, since many must be left to guard the other slaves, who are mutinous. You, and you—" He picked out the four biggest ones. "GO at once and join the search. I will stay here with the others."

It nearly worked. The four took a hesitant step or two, and then one paused and said doubtfully,

"But, my lord, it is forbidden that we leave our posts, for any reason. Any reason at all, my lord! The Lord Cond would slay us if we left this place."

"And you fear the Lord Cond more than you do me," said Treon philosophically. "Ah, well. I understand."

He stepped out, full into the light.

A gasp went up, and then a startled yell. The three men from inside had come out armed only with swords, but the two sentries had their shock-weapons. One of them shrieked,

"It is a demon, who speaks with Treon's voice!"

And the two black weapons started up.

Behind them, Stark fired two silent bolts in quick

succession, and the men fell, safely out of the way for hours. Then he leaped for the door.

He collided with two men who were doing the same thing. The third had turned to hold Treon off with his sword until they were safely inside.

Seeing that Treon, who was unarmed, was in danger of being spitted on the man's point, Stark fired between the two lunging bodies as he fell, and brought the guard down. Then he was involved in a thrashing tangle of arms and legs, and a lucky blow jarred the shock-weapon out of his hand.

Treon added himself to the fray. Pleasuring in his new strength, he caught one man by the neck and pulled him off. The guards were big men, and powerful, and they fought desperately. Stark was bruised and bleeding from a cut mouth before he could get in a finishing blow.

Someone rushed past him into the doorway. Treon yelled. Out of the tail of his eyes Stark saw the Lhari sitting dazed on the ground. The door was closing.

Stark hunched up his shoulders and sprang.

HE HIT the heavy panel with a jar that nearly knocked him breathless. It slammed open, and there was a cry of pain and the sound of someone falling. Stark burst through, to find the last of the guards rolling every which way over the floor. But one rolled over onto his feet again, drawing his sword as he rose. He had not had time before.

Stark continued his rush without stopping. He plunged headlong into the man before the point was clear of the scabbard, bore him over and down, and finished the man off with savage efficiency.

He leaped to his feet, breathing hard, spitting blood out of his mouth, and looked around the control room. But the others had fled, obviously to raise the warning.

The mechanism was simple. It was contained in a large black metal oblong about the size and shape of a coffin, equipped with grids and lenses and dials. It hummed softly to itself, but what its source of power was Stark did not know. Perhaps those same cosmic rays, harnessed to a different use.

He closed what seemed to be a master switch, and the humming stopped, and the flickering light died out of the lenses. He picked up the slain guard's sword and carefully wrecked everything that was breakable. Then he went outside again.

Treon was standing up, shaking his head. He smiled ruefully.

"It seems that strength alone is not enough," he said. "One must have skill as well."

"The barriers are down," said Stark. "The way is clear."

Treon nodded, and went with him back into the sea. This time both carried shock weapons taken from the guards—six in all, with Egil's. Total armament for war.

As they forged swiftly through the red depths, Stark asked, "What of the people of Shuruun? How will they fight?"

Treon answered, "Those of Malthor's breed will stand for the Lhari. They must, for all their hope is there. The others will wait, until they see which side is safest. They would rise against the Lhari if they dared, for we have brought them only fear in their lifetimes. But they will wait, and see."

Stark nodded. He did not speak again.

They passed over the brooding city, and Stark thought of Egil and of Malthor who were part of that silence now, drifting slowly through the empty streets where the little currents took them, wrapped in their shrouds of dim fire.

He thought of Zareth sleeping in the hall of kings, and his eyes held a cold, cruel light.

They swooped down over the slave barracks. Treon remained on watch outside. Stark went in, taking with him the extra weapons.

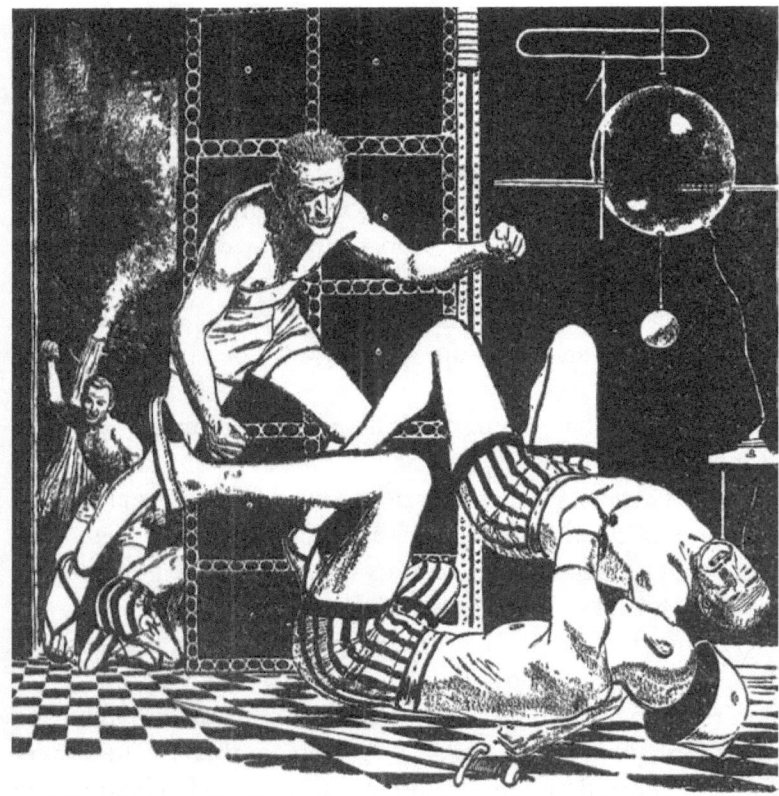

The slaves still slept. Some of them dreamed, and moaned in their dreaming, and others might have been dead, with their hollow faces white as skulls.

Slaves. One hundred and four, counting the women.

Stark shouted out to them, and they woke, starting up on their pallets, their eyes full of terror. Then they saw who it was that called them, standing collarless and armed, and there was a great surging and a clamor that stilled as Stark shouted again, demanding silence. This time Helvi's voice echoed his. The tall barbarian had wakened from his drugged sleep.

Stark told them, very briefly, all that happened.

"You are freed from the collar," he said. "This day you can survive or die as men, and not slaves." He paused, then

Stark burst through.

asked, "Who will go with me into Shuruun?"

They answered with one voice, the voice of the Lost Ones, who saw the red pall of death begin to lift from over them. The Lost Ones, who had found hope again.

Stark laughed. He was happy. He gave the extra weapons to Helvi and three others that he chose, and Helvi looked into his eyes and laughed too.

Treon spoke from the open door. "They are coming."

STARK gave Helvi quick instructions and darted out, taking with him one of the other men. With Treon, they hid among the shrubbery of the garden that was outside the hall, patterned and beautiful, swaying its lifeless brilliance in the lazy drifts of fire.

The guards came. Twenty of them, tall armed men, to turn out the slaves for another period of labor, dragging the useless stones. And the hidden weapons spoke with their silent tongues.

Eight of the guards fell inside the hall. Nine of them went down outside. Ten of the slaves died with blazing collars before the remaining three were overcome.

Now there were twenty swords among ninety-four slaves, counting the women.

They left the city and rose up over the dreaming forest, a flight of white ghosts with flames in their hair, coming back from the red dusk and the silence to find the light again.

Light, and vengeance.

The first pale glimmer of dawn was sifting through the clouds as they came up among the rocks below the castle of the Lhari. Stark left them and went like a shadow up the tumbled cliffs to where he had hidden his gun on the night he had first come to Shuruun. Nothing stirred. The fog lifted up from the sea like a vapor of blood, and the face of Venus was still dark. Only the high clouds were touched with pearl.

Stark returned to the others. He gave one of his shock-weapons to a swamp-lander with a cold madness in his eyes. Then he spoke a few final words to Helvi and went back with Treon under the surface of the sea.

Treon led the way. He went along the face of the submerged cliff, and presently he touched Stark's arm and pointed to where a round mouth opened in the rock.

"It was made long ago," said Treon, "so that the Lhari and

their slavers might come and go and not be seen. Come—and be very quiet."

They swam into the tunnel mouth, and down the dark way that lay beyond, until the lift of the floor brought them out of the sea. Then they felt their way silently along, stopping now and again to listen.

Surprise was their only hope. Treon had said that with the two of them they might succeed. More men would surely be discovered, and meet a swift end at the hands of the guards.

Stark hoped Treon was right.

They came to a blank wall of dressed stone. Treon leaned his weight against one side, and a great block swung slowly around on a central pivot. Guttering torchlight came through the crack. By it Stark could see that the room beyond was empty.

They stepped through, and as they did so, a servant in bright silks came yawning into the room with a fresh torch to replace the one that was dying.

He stopped in mid-step, his eyes widening. He dropped the torch. His mouth opened to shape a scream, but no sound came, and Stark remembered that these servants were tongueless—to prevent them from telling what they saw or heard in the castle, Treon said.

The man spun about and fled, down a long dim-lit hall. Stark ran him down without effort. He struck once with the barrel of his gun, and the man fell and was still.

Treon came up. His face had a look almost of exaltation, a queer shining of the eyes that made Stark shiver. He led on, through a series of empty rooms, all somber black, and they met no one else for a while.

He stopped at last before a small door of burnished gold. He looked at Stark once, and nodded, and thrust the panels open and stepped through.

CHAPTER TWELVE

THEY STOOD INSIDE THE vast echoing hall that stretched away into darkness until it seemed there was no end to it. The cluster of silver lamps burned as before, and within their circle of radiance the Lhari started up from their places and stared at the strangers who had come in through their private door.

Cond, and Arel with her hands idle in her lap. Bor, pummeling the little two-headed dragon to make it hiss and snap, laughing at its impotence. Varra, stroking the winged creature on her wrist, testing with her white finger the sharpness of its beak. And the old woman, with a scrap of fat meat halfway to her mouth.

They had stopped, frozen, in the midst of these actions. And Treon walked slowly into the light.

"Do you know me?" he said.

A strange shivering ran through them. Now, as before, the old woman spoke first, her eyes glittering with a look as rapacious as her appetite.

"You are Treon," she said, and her whole vast body shook.

The name went crying and whispering off around the dark walls, *Treon! Treon! Treon!* Cond leaped forward, touching his cousin's straight strong body with hands that trembled.

"You have found it," he said. "The secret."

"Yes." Treon lifted his silver head and laughed, a beautiful ringing bell-note that sang from the echoing corners. "I found it, and it's gone, smashed, beyond your reach forever. Egil is dead, and the day of the Lhari is done."

There was a long, long silence, and then the old woman whispered, *"You lie!"*

Treon turned to Stark.

"Ask him, the stranger who came bearing doom upon his forehead. Ask him if I lie."

Cond's face became something less than human. He made a queer crazed sound and flung himself at Treon's throat.

Bor screamed suddenly. He alone was not much concerned with the finding or the losing of the secret, and he alone seemed to realize the significance of Stark's presence. He screamed, looking at the big dark man, and went rushing off down the hall, crying for the guard as he went, and the echoes roared and racketed. He fought open the great doors and ran out, and as he did so the sound of fighting came through from the compound.

The slaves, with their swords and clubs, with their stones and shards of rock, had come over the wall from the cliffs.

Stark had moved forward, but Treon did not need his help. He had got his hands around Cond's throat, and he was smiling. Stark did not disturb him.

The old woman was talking, cursing, commanding, choking on her own apoplectic breath. Arel began to laugh. She did not move, and her hands remained limp and open in her lap. She laughed and laughed, and Varra looked at Stark and hated him.

"You're a fool, wild man," she said. "You would not take what I offered you, so you shall have nothing—only death."

She slipped the hood from her creature and set it straight at Stark. Then she drew a knife from her girdle and plunged it into Treon's side.

TREON reeled back. His grip loosened and Cond tore away, half throttled, raging, his mouth flecked with foam. He drew his short sword and staggered in upon Treon.

Furious wings beat and thundered around Stark's head, and talons were clawing for his eyes. He reached up with his left hand and caught the brute by one leg and held it. Not long, but long enough to get one clear shot at Cond that dropped him in his tracks. Then he snapped the falcon's neck.

He flung the creature at Varra's feet, and picked up the gun again. The guards were rushing into the hall now at the lower end, and he began to fire at them.

Treon was sitting on the floor. Blood was coming in a steady trickle from his side, but he had the shock-weapon in his hands, and he was still smiling.

There was a great boiling roar of noise from outside. Men were fighting there, killing, dying, screaming their triumph or their pain. The echoes raged within the hall, and the noise of Stark's gun was like a hissing thunder. The guards, armed only with swords, went down like ripe wheat before the sickle, but there were many of them, too many for Stark and Treon to hold for long.

The old woman shrieked and shrieked, and was suddenly still.

Helvi burst in through the press, with a knot of collared slaves. The fight dissolved into a whirling chaos. Stark threw his gun away. He was afraid now of hitting his own men. He caught up a sword from a fallen guard and began to hew his way to the barbarian.

Suddenly Treon cried his name. He leaped aside, away from the man he was fighting, and saw Varra fall with the dagger still in her hand. She had come up behind him to stab, and Treon had seen and pressed the trigger stud just in time.

For the first time, there were tears in Treon's eyes.

A sort of sickness came over Stark. There was something horrible in this spectacle of a family destroying itself. He was too much the savage to be sentimental over Varra, but all the same he could not bear to look at Treon for a while.

Presently he found himself back to back with Helvi, and as they swung their swords—the shock weapons had been discarded for the same reason as Stark's gun—Helvi panted,

"It has been a good fight, my brother. We cannot win, but we can have a good death, which is better than slavery."

It looked as though Helvi was right.

The slaves, unfortunately, weakened by their long confinement, worn out by overwork, were being beaten back. The tide turned, and Stark was swept with it out into the compound, fighting stubbornly.

The great gate stood open. Beyond it stood the people of Shuruun, watching, hanging back—as Treon had said, they would wait and see.

In the forefront, leaning on his stick, stood Larrabee the Earthman.

Stark cut his way free of the press. He leaped up onto the wall and stood there, breathing hard, sweating, bloody, with a dripping sword in his hand. He waved it, shouting down to the men of Shuruun.

"What are you waiting for, you scuts, you women? The Lhari are dead, the Lost Ones are freed—must we of Earth do all your work for you?"

And he looked straight at Larrabee.

Larrabee stared back, his dark suffering eyes full of a bitter mirth. "Oh, well," he said in English. "Why not?"

He threw back his head and laughed, and the bitterness was gone. He voiced a high, shrill rebel yell and lifted his stick like a cudgel, limping toward the gate, and the men of Shuruun gave tongue and followed him.

After that, it was soon over.

THEY found Bor's body in the stable pens, where he had hidden when the fighting started. The dragons, maddened by the smell of the blood, had slain him very quickly.

Helvi had come through alive, and Larrabee, who had kept himself carefully out of harm's way after he had started the men of Shuruun on their attack. Nearly half the slaves were dead, and the rest wounded. Of those who had served the Lhari, few were left.

Stark went back into the great hall. He walked slowly, for he was very weary, and where he set his foot there was a bloody print, and his arms were red to the elbows, and his breast was splashed with the redness. Treon watched him come, and smiled, nodding.

"It is as I said. And I have outlived them all."

Arel had stopped laughing at last. She had made no move to run away, and the tide of battle had rolled over her and drowned her unaware. The old woman lay still, a mountain of inert flesh upon her bed. Her hand still clutched a ripe fruit, clutched convulsively in the moment of death, the red juice dripping through her fingers.

"Now I am going, too," said Treon, "and I am well content. With me goes the last of our rotten blood, and Venus will be the cleaner for it. Bury my body deep, stranger with the fierce eyes. I would not have it looked on after this."

He sighed and fell forward.

Bor's little dragon crept whimpering out from its hiding place under the old woman's bed and scurried away down the hall, trailing its dragging rope.

STARK leaned on the taffrail, watching the dark mass of Shuruun recede into the red mists.

The decks were crowded with the outland slaves, going home. The Lhari were gone, the Lost Ones freed forever, and Shuruun was now only another port on the Red Sea. Its people would still be wolf's-heads and pirates, but that was natural and as it should be. The black evil was gone.

Stark was glad to see the last of it. He would be glad also to see the last of the Red Sea.

The off shore wind set the ship briskly down the gulf. Stark thought of Larrabee, left behind with his dreams of winter snows and city streets and women with dainty feet. It seemed that he had lived too long in Shuruun, and had lost the courage to leave it.

"Poor Larrabee," he said to Helvi, who was standing near him. "He'll die in the mud, still cursing it."

Someone laughed behind him. He heard a limping step on the deck and turned to see Larrabee coming toward him.

"Changed my mind at the last minute," Larrabee said. "I've been below, lest I should see my muddy brats and be tempted to change it again." He leaned beside Stark, shaking his head. "Ah, well, they'll do nicely without me. I'm an old man, and I've a right to choose my own place to die in. I'm going back to Earth, with you."

Stark glanced at him. "I'm not going to Earth."

Larrabee sighed. "No. No, I suppose you're not. After all, you're no Earthman, really, except for an accident of blood. Where are you going?"

"I don't know. Away from Venus, but I don't know yet where."

Larrabee's dark eyes surveyed him shrewdly. "'A restless, cold-eyed tiger of a man, that's what Varra said. He's lost something, she said. He'll look for it all his life, and never find it.'"

After that there was silence. The red fog wrapped them, and the wind rose and sent them scudding before it

Then, faint and far off, there came a moaning wail, a sound like broken chanting that turned Stark's flesh cold.

All on board heard it. They listened, utterly silent, their eyes wide, and somewhere a woman began to weep.

Stark shook himself. "It's only the wind," he said roughly,

"in the rocks by the strait."

The sound rose and fell, weary, infinitely mournful, and the part of Stark that was N'Chaka said that he lied. It was not the wind that keened so sadly through the mists. It was the voices of the Lost Ones who were forever lost—Zareth, sleeping in the hall of kings, and all the others who would never leave the dreaming city and the forest, never find the light again.

Stark shivered, and turned away, watching the leaping fires of the strait sweep toward them.

THE END

If you've enjoyed this book, you will not want to miss these terrific titles…

ARMCHAIR SCI-FI & HORROR DOUBLE NOVELS, $12.95 each

D-1   **THE GALAXY RAIDERS** by William P. McGivern
SPACE STATION #1 by Frank Belknap Long

D-2   **THE PROGRAMMED PEOPLE** by Jack Sharkey
SLAVES OF THE CRYSTAL BRAIN by William Carter Sawtelle

D-3   **YOU'RE ALL ALONE** by Fritz Leiber
THE LIQUID MAN by Bernard C. Gilford

D-4   **CITADEL OF THE STAR LORDS** by Edmond Hamilton
VOYAGE TO ETERNITY by Milton Lesser

D-5   **IRON MEN OF VENUS** by Don Wilcox
THE MAN WITH ABSOLUTE MOTION by Noel Loomis

D-6   **WHO SOWS THE WIND…** by Rog Phillips
THE PUZZLE PLANET by Robert A. W. Lowndes

D-7   **PLANET OF DREAD** by Murray Leinster
TWICE UPON A TIME by Charles L. Fontenay

D-8   **THE TERROR OUT OF SPACE** by Dwight V. Swain
QUEST OF THE GOLDEN APE by Ivar Jorgensen and Adam Chase

D-9   **SECRET OF MARRACOTT DEEP** by Henry Slesar
PAWN OF THE BLACK FLEET by Mark Clifton.

D-10   **BEYOND THE RINGS OF SATURN** by Robert Moore Williams
A MAN OBSESSED by Alan E. Nourse

ARMCHAIR SCIENCE FICTION CLASSICS, $12.95 each

C-1   **THE GREEN MAN**
by Harold M. Sherman

C-2   **A TRACE OF MEMORY**
By Keith Laumer

C-3   **INTO PLUTONIAN DEPTHS**
by Stanton A. Coblentz

ARMCHAIR MASTERS OF SCIENCE FICTION SERIES, $16.95 each

M-1   **MASTERS OF SCIENCE FICTION, Vol. One**
Bryce Walton: "Dark of the Moon" and other tales

M-2   **MASTERS OF SCIENCE FICTION, Vol. Two**
Jerome Bixby: "One Way Street" and other tales

If you've enjoyed this book, you will not want to miss these terrific titles…

ARMCHAIR SCI-FI & HORROR DOUBLE NOVELS, $12.95 each

D-11 **PERIL OF THE STARMEN** by Kris Neville
THE FORGOTTEN PLANET by Murray Leinster

D-12 **THE STAR LORD** by Boyd Ellanby
CAPTIVES OF THE FLAME by Samuel R. Delany

D-13 **MEN OF THE MORNING STAR** by Edmond Hamilton
PLANET FOR PLUNDER by Hal Clement and Sam Merwin, Jr.

D-14 **ICE CITY OF THE GORGON** by Chester S. Geier and Richard Shaver
WHEN THE WORLD TOTTERED by Lester del Rey

D-15 **WORLDS WITHOUT END** by Clifford D. Simak
THE LAVENDER VINE OF DEATH by Don Wilcox

D-16 **SHADOW ON THE MOON** by Joe Gibson
ARMAGEDDON EARTH by Geoff St. Reynard

D-17 **THE GIRL WHO LOVED DEATH** by Paul W. Fairman
SLAVE PLANET by Laurence M. Janifer

D-18 **SECOND CHANCE** by J. F. Bone
MISSION TO A DISTANT STAR by Frank Belknap Long

D-19 **THE SYNDIC** by C. M. Kornbluth
FLIGHT TO FOREVER by Poul Anderson

D-20 **SOMEWHERE I'LL FIND YOU** by Milton Lesser
THE TIME ARMADA by Fox B. Holden

ARMCHAIR SCIENCE FICTION CLASSICS, $12.95 each

C-4 **CORPUS EARTHLING**
by Louis Charbonneau

C-5 **THE TIME DISSOLVER**
by Jerry Sohl

C-6 **WEST OF THE SUN**
by Edgar Pangborn

ARMCHAIR SCI-FI & HORROR GEMS SERIES, $12.95 each

G-1 **SCIENCE FICTION GEMS, Vol. One**
Isaac Asimov and others

G-2 **HORROR GEMS, Vol. One**
Carl Jacobi and others